ZANY!

A Father-Son Odyssey

ZANY!

A Father–Son Odyssey

Jim Gold

Full Court Press
Englewood Cliffs, New Jersey

First Edition

Copyright © 2012 by Jim Gold

Published in the United States of America
by Full Court Press, 601 Palisade Avenue
Englewood Cliffs, NJ 07632
www.fullcourtpressnj.com

ISBN 978-0-9609948-0-9
Library of Congress Control No. 2011945584

Editing and Book Design by Barry Sheinkopf
for Bookshapers (www.bookshapers.com)

Cover photo of Mount Ararat
courtesy www.istockphoto.com
Author photo by Barry Sheinkopf
Colophon by Liz Sedlack

To Bernice
woman of my dreams,
anchor of my adventures

LOST

1

WHAT MAKES A LUNA TICK?

MARTHA WAS PREPARING COFFEE and baked doughnuts of the Austrian variety for the violinist Dr. Zoltan Zany.

The legendary concert artist sat in his living room armchair facing the window. Outside, in the garden, sparrows chirped a morning fugue, and a bee hovered above a red rose, buzzing in B-flat.

Martha stood before the kitchen stove. "Hot and fresh," she called. "Doctor, are you ready?"

A sonorous grunt of affirmation sounded from the living room. Martha carried her serving tray across the Turkish rug, placed it next to the master, and rearranged the Viennese delicacies. She poured coffee into the doctor's favorite Herendware cup, purchased six years before in Hungary after his performance of Lalo's *Symphonie Espagnol* with the Budapest Philharmonic.

Zany sniffed the aroma, dipped his pinky in the dark Columbian brew, stirred thoroughly, lifted the cup to his lips, closed his eyes, and sipped slowly.

"Aah," he sighed, "those Columbians know what they're doing. Delicious! *Koszonom szepen, danke shoen,* and *aufwiedersehen*. Martha, when your culinary creations fill my stomach, my heart beats faster, my brain improves, my fingers fill with blood, then fly in a 'Moto Perpetuo' of Paganini madness. Caffeine, my friend, you are my Paganini 'Caprice.' Niccolo, how I remember our good times together. Were you really possessed by the devil?"

Zany bit into a doughnut flank. Munching vigorously, his white, bushy handlebar mustache trembled. As the sugar entered his veins, visions of yodeling Tyrolean cows and Alpine trumpets filled his imagination. He drifted from Switzerland to the Eurasian steppes and rode his horse through the high grass on the Hungarian Hortobagy Plain in his ancestral homeland. Another doughnut, and he lay, languid, lazy, and stuffed, on a Lake Balaton beach, gazing at a blue magyar sky.

"*Mein Doktor*, look outside," Martha cried. "Clouds have fled. The sun is shining. Plant nutrients sing in happy comfort. It's a new day!"

Dr. Zany leaned back his armchair. He picked up the *New York Times* lying on the floor to his right, turned to the weather section, closed his eyes, and fell asleep again.

He'd been sitting in that arm chair almost a year.

Martha nudged him. He blinked. Consciousness returned. He opened his eyes, pushed himself forward in his seat, and said with resignation, "My favorite and only servant, sunbeams cannot dispel my confusion. Is today tomorrow? Is it the day before yesterday? Or the morning after the night before yesterday? I consulted my ankle. It didn't know."

Martha stepped away, picked up a napkin from Zany's tray, and began dusting the furniture. The doctor's voice followed her from living room to kitchen and back. "Tell me about your mother again," she called out.

Zany curled the white ends of his mustache. "Should I blame Mama Zany for my present state?" he asked. "Her goulash helped promote my concert career. But now, after months of sitting at home, my retreat has descended into existential nothingness. Mama said such visits from the Weltanschauung powers of misery would occur. Yet the blues and greens hit me all at once. Retirement may not be my way. True, I luxuriate in this armchair, but nevertheless, with such a sedentary existence and spirit sinking so close to lower Hades, will it ever rise again? The great Paganini himself claimed, before writing his *D major Violin Concerto*, that depression precedes creation. Yet sadly, although I've been near bottom during these past months, I've created nothing."

Hoping to stimulate his tired brain, Zany shook his head vigorously. A few stale ideas fell out. Somewhat cleansed, he felt better. Turning to the wall, he said to one board in particular, "*I can find no reason to rise!*

"Ah, but what a career I had! Concertizing in 113 countries and on six continents. Or was it seven? Even Antarctica! My agent, Sammy Blickenstein, was too cheap to hire an orchestra on that freezing day, so I played the Brahms violin concerto on an ice floe with no accompaniment. After a short intermission, I followed it with the Bach "Chaconne." Penguins loved it. Ice floes clapped, and moonbeams seemed to coo, creating a lunar symphony I'd never before heard. 'Well,' I said, as my boat left for Tierra del Fuego in Argentina, 'the hell with Sammy! Those arctic birds were polite. They paid full price, too.'"

Zany cleared his throat. He shifted in his armchair, coughed into his napkin, and took another sip of coffee. "My travels frightened Mama Magyar. She never approved of them. Growing up in the Hungarian-Serbian town of Szentendre, she lived

in the artistic shadow of the potter Margaret Mezokoszonem-
nagyonszeppen Kovacs; this created early childhood traumas
that haunted her after the transmigration of her soul and immi-
gration of her lithe body to the Bronx. She suffered from agro-
phobia, claustrophbia, phlebitis of the gastrointestinal porceloid
track, and utcaphobia—a fear of Hungarian streets. No doctor
could cure or even find her diseases. Nevertheless, she blamed
all her ailments on my travels." Zany sighed, spat a whomp of
phlegm across the room in disgust, and gnashed his teeth; his
long white hair fluttered. "Am I lost now in my retirement chair
because of *her*? Or has the guilt over forgetting my father's
corpse at the funeral parlor not been assuaged?"

Zany's face reddened as memories returned; emerging rage
seared his forehead. Those had not been happy years.

"Martha, does Zoltan mean 'Sultan'? Mother named me
that, but I don't know why. Was her brain soft?"

Martha began dusting his head sympathetically. "Do not
worry," she counseled. "The road ahead is full of light. Unknown post-armchair glory awaits you."

Zany raised his powerful right bowing arm, opened his
right hand, and looked straight into his palm. Suddenly, he
slapped his right cheek. "How *ungrateful* of me!" he shouted.
"Vilify my sacred mother! Her shamanistic aura filled my
childhood days with wonder. Her compassionate warning,
'Never bring children up like a truck,' still resonates in my
mind. She worshiped perfection. She strove to perfect her little Zoltan by forcing me to practice violin six hours a day. At
night I slept with my violin. I caressed the G and D strings as
I dozed off, and even learned a Mozart sonata in my sleep.
However, such childhood intensity habits have long-term ef-
fects. As you see, in my present armchair mode, I am physi-

cally immobile and mentally stagnant. Could there be hidden meaning in this paralysis, a cosmic sign? I yearn for epistemological certitude."

Rays of sunlight slipped through the Venetian blinds and fell in diagonal patterns across the Turkish carpet. Martha fumbled with the wall plug and pushed the straws of her broom into the electric socket, cleaning its interior. "Meaning is important. Direction is vital." Emphasizing her point, she straightened up, raised her broom in the medieval Order of Teutonic Knights of Jerusalem diagonal spear position, and, in martial tone, trumpeted, *"Ordo domus Sanctæ Mariæ Theutonicorum Hierosolymitanorum!"* Bending towards Zany's right ear, she whispered Three Questions: *"Doktor*, why were you born? Why are you here? What is your purpose?"

Zany shook his head. "Martha, I'm disappointed. You have worked for me ten years, and you still don't know why?" He waved his hand, conducting his thoughts in three-quarter time. "My goal has always been self-elevation. Even now, in my static condition, I fervently wish I could leave my armchair and cross the living room. Perhaps I might even stand at the staircase, and *rise* to the second floor!"

Martha glanced at a cluster of cobwebs on the ceiling. Spying their creator, a small black spider hanging from one of the webs, she briefly considered the nature of Tarentella dancing in Naples. After her nimble mind had filtered notions of Platonic idealism, Marxist dialectical materialism, the imprecations of Vladimir Lenin, and faux-Yiddish dialectics of Heinrich von Tubbehoffenspiegel, she turned to Dr. Zany, and said, "I appreciate purposeful thinking about the Ends of Man, and the sturdiness of your teleological philosophy. What are your terms?" She swatted the spider.

Zany remembered his performance of the Bruch violin concerto before one thousand camels and their riders at St. Catherine's Monastery at the foot of Mt. Sinai. Imagining Moses holding a burning bush high in his right hand, the doctor pushed himself up from his armchair, stamped his foot on the floor, and in stentorian voice exclaimed: "I speak in *biblical* terms!"

Then he sank back.

Martha's question had forced him to consider his future. He remained silent, cupping his chin in puzzlement.

A few hours later, he asked, "Martha, do you think Mother and Father Zany will join my celestial adventure?"

"Of course," she replied. "Everyone likes a heavenly quest. But, *mein Doktor*, there are obstacles. First you must free yourself of lassitude. *Ausgeschnel* your *sitzfleisch zeitgeist*. Empower yourself. Get up!"

Zany bowed his head in agreement. "I know," he said. "The mystery of motivation. Reach the second floor. Before such elevation is attained, I must rise again."

2

DREAMS

WHAT WOULD YOU LIKE for breakfast, *mein Doktor?*" Martha asked. Rays of cascading sunlight had brightened the kitchen.

Raising his bedtime sunglasses, Zany pondered the question. He leaned hard on his thinking leg while his right thumb, calloused from years of violin bowing, slowly stroked his magyar nose.

Martha waited impatiently, tapping an Austrian waltz on her frying pan.

"What do you *need?*"

"A dream. A big one!"

Zany lifted a handkerchief from his pocket and wiped a tear from his eye. "A land without dreams is worse than a desert."

"Then dream!" Martha declared. "Indeed, life without dreams is unbearable. So is death. But life, especially for you, my *doktor, is* a dream. Dreaming is part of your shamanic tradition and Hungarian heritage."

Zoltan's shoulders sagged in resignation. Beads of perspiration broke out on his forehead as thoughts of his recent concert tour of Jordan rose in his mind. He remembered the Nabatean ruins of Petra, where he had performed the *Camel Violin Concerto* by the Ma'anian oud virtuoso Ahmad Al Aswara before ten thousand swaying fans. Wiping off the sweat, he sighed, "Where did I lose my dream? How do I find another? Shall I invent one? Are dreams born of the same Void from which the Music Master created the world?"

He continued his inner journey along the twisted wadis of his dried- up past. "Once, my concert performances excited me. But now they have reached their apotheosis. I sit here faded and finished. Where are my new challenges? Can one weave new cloth from old wool?"

"Yes, your skills have been perfected," Martha remarked. "You've gone as far as you can go. Sleeping in the old life is healthy during transitions. But this somnambulance is temporary. New worlds lie ahead."

Zany considered his struggle. The face of discouragement rose before him. Opposites clashed: an internal battleground soaked in bloody choices of absence or nothingness.

Yet hope glimmered: "It means working harder, sinking deeper into what I've got," Zany declared. "Give up the horizontal. Pursue the vertical. Depth instead of width. To regain my freshness, I need not fondle the same old tit. On to new breasts! But where? When Captain Marvel said, 'Shazzam!' did he mean *me?* Perhaps I'll write a new Zany composition."

"What would you compose?" asked Martha.

Indeed, what sperm cells was the Music Master carrying on His silver tray today? Would notes and majestic sound even be part of the doctor's future? Only a rooster could tell.

A rooster! Zany turned to face his garden. Bees and gnats flew in all directions.

3

LIFE OF ATTILA

Attila Zany, a brilliant Linguistic student, had graduated from New York's Maritime High School the previous June at age sixteen. Two months later, after accepting admission to Western Bustard University, he drove cross country to Copper Gulch Country, Colorado. There, in the college town of Springing Tree ten thousand feet above sea level, he settled into his dormitory single, spread his books on the floor, nailed a Hungarian cannon poster on the wall, lay down on the fresh linen of his new bed, and fell into a deep sleep of happy exhaustion.

Two days later, waking refreshed and exhilarated, he took an exploratory walk around town. Passing beneath a canopy of leafy maples, he spied a grocery selling fresh vegetables. Picking up some tomatoes and munching them carefully, he peered into the window of a clothing store specializing in camping equipment; beside the store stood a weapons disposal unit, followed by a book store featuring a sale of Karl Marx's *Das Capital* edited by Leslie Lenin, great-grandson of Friedrich Engels. Attila went inside, purchased a paperback copy, sat down on the curb, opened the book, lay back to read a few pages, and soon fell asleep on the sidewalk. The high altitude with its thin oxygenation had slowed his bodily and mental processes, quieted his emotions, especially his violent streak, and given him a headache.

However, the rarified atmosphere also facilitated etymological analysis, creating subtle linguistic shifts, not only in his command of classical Latin and Greek, but in his continued study of Ugoritic, Phoenician, Akkadian, and Sumerian. It was in fact during that first semester at Bustard, his so- called "Sidewalk Period," as he dozed on cement, that Attila formulated his Theory of Linguistic Connection, the notion that ancient Sumerian and modern Finno-Ugric came from the same linguistic family. "Ur," as in Abraham's *Ur of the Chaldeans*, and the biblo-Chaldean city of Erech (Ur-ech), had names closely related to their modern Hungarian equivalent *Ur*, meaning "master" or "mister." Attila practiced his developing linguistic skills on his cell phone, calling his father *Ur Zany* and bowing before the technology in deep respect.

The lad had borrowed many of these ideas from *Origin of the Hungarian Nation,* by the Floridian scholarette Ida Bobula. Several months later, as mastery of his skills grew, he was discovered by Dr. Babril Tsupalensky, Rector of Bustard University's Linguistics Department, who offered him a full linguistic scholarship.

With new funds available, Attila rented a mountain cabin. He spent the next four years surrounded by glorious pine trees, bears, skunks, and birds. Hoping to improve his fluency in ancient languages, he spoke Akkadian to passing bears, using phrases like "How Ur you?" or "Give me Ur hand." The bears observed him strangely, and their blank response convinced him that better communication skills between bears and humans were needed.

During this "cabin period," he wrote *Grammar of Ursaline Linguistics*, which became a best-seller among forest rangers and environmentally conscious Coloradians. Page 16 of the book, filled with action verbs, was adopted by leaders of the "Free the Bears" movement. By assiduously studying its contents as their guide, Podunk Sleswick, Joe "Pebbles" Podushevsky, and Ellen Estretch organized an Ursine March on Washington. Attila's ursaline verb forms enabled them to speak directly to bears. Alas, the march failed to materialize after the two leaders were clawed to death during a bear consciousness-raising session.

Attila, having spent most of his four college years in his cabin, asked himself one month before graduation, "Where do I go from here?" Answers to this question along with his story of personal transformation can be found in his autobiography, *A Bustard Among Men:*

It started during my last year at Bustard. What I would do after I graduated? What path would I take? Self-discovery was my goal; I wanted to understand the Me inside me.

One day, in a meditative mood, I took a walk on one of the many mountain trails outside town. Pines, sedimentary rocks, sparkling granite beauties, sprinkled and popped on the marked trail. The rising sun threw spears of flashing light across my path.

Suddenly, a heard a gunshot! Running further up the path, I heard another. I spied a man sitting in a tree, rifle in hand, aiming at the ground. Bang! When he saw me, he aimed at me. Bang! A bullet whizzed past me. Then another and another. Luckily, he always missed.

We soon became friends. That tall, slender man, balanced precariously on a branch, wore a buckskin shirt, leather pants, an Indian feather behind his ear, and heavy work boots. A red beard covered the right side of his face, and a gray cowboy hat, with a plastic eagle perched above it, sat on his head.

He lowered his gun. "Who are you?"

"Attila Zany."

He raised his gun, pointed it at my chest, and looked me over. "Sounds Hunnish to me." *The man squinted, waited a moment, but eventually lowered his weapon.* "The only Zany I know is Brunhilde Zany. She lives down in Cleaver Creek."

"That's my mother."

"Your ma?"

"Yup. After I got into Bustard, I left New Jersey. Ma wanted to be near me. So she moved to Colorado to keep our relationship close."

"You're a Bustard U. guy? Out here we call them U Bustards. Four years ago some Bustards from the Animal Rights Department hired me as a wildlife lab technician. I like animals. They said to me, 'Bob, we're doing a study of rattlesnake bites. You're a winner with a gun. Want to kill snakes for us? I said, 'Sure, why not?' That's why folks call me 'Rattlesnake.'"

"Fitting."

"Right. I'm an aural kind of guy. I like sounds, rattling sounds—tin can rattle, coconut rattle, snake rattle, death rattle, anything that rattles. I like killing things, too. When my lab job ended, my life wasn't going anywhere. I looked into my heart and decided to pursue my deepest interest. So I bought a gun, came to the mountains, sat down by the roadside, and shot rattlesnakes. Been doing it three years now. A good life until six months ago. . . . I ran out of snakes. The peace and quiet *nearly killed me. Then I decided to take control of my life. I took my money out of the Denver bank, headed for Toys R Us, and bought out their baby rattles. I've been shooting rattles ever since."*

"Expensive hobby."

"Hobby? Shooting isn't a hobby. It's a calling! When I realized the importance of it, and the pressure it put me under, I could hardly stand it. I even thought about killing people! I tried a few times, got arrested, ended up in prison. But after a year, the warden gave up on me. 'You're too violent for prison,' he said. 'I'm putting you on the street where you can do some good.' I've been out ever since.

"But my interest in shooting people evaporated. No one smiled at me when I shot them. I like a good reception. I like smiles. If folks don't appreciate you, life's no fun. So now I only shoot snakes, when there are any, and rattles when there ain't."

"Did you ever meet my ma?"

"Sure did. She's some babe. What a sombrero! Does she ever take that thing off?"

"Hasn't for years. She's ashamed of her cerebralectomy. The doctor started but never finished. . . ." I shifted to one leg. Reflecting further on my childhood, I added, "Rattlesnake, you're making me homesick. Maybe I'll visit her."

"Mothers're like that. Mine sure was until I shot her lemon pie full of holes." Rattlesnake raised his gun, aimed at one of the broken toy rattles lying under the pine tree, and pulled the trigger. The pop of the gunshot rattled and ricocheted throughout the canyon. "It's always good to visit your ma. To my knowledge, she's still living in Schizoid House."

"...*She took that name from her sorority house. I've never liked it. It demeans her talents.*"

"*Well, maybe, but as I said, it's always good to visit your mother.*"

"*Okay, Rattlesnake. I'll do it.*"

"*Good boy.*" *Rattlesnake smiled.* " *Here, take this.*" *He handed Attila his weapon.* "*It's a present.*"

"*Oh, I can't do that. What about your—your calling?*"

"*Someone else is calling. I'm tired of killing. I'm retiring. No rattlesnakes left. Even the baby rattles are nearly gone. Shooting has run its course. I don't need it anymore. I'm passing it on to you. Here's some advice: Never hurt a human soul. Hurting is mean, real mean. I never hurt anybody. Kill them if you like, but don't you ever hurt them.*"

Rattlesnake got up from his rock, brushed off his pants, and walked down the mountain.

ATTILA VISITS MAMA ZANY

ATTILA KEPT HIS WORD. He visited Mama Brunhilde Zany at her mountain hideaway, a log cabin high in the Tetrahymenic Peptide Chain, a group of mountains in the backyard named after her favorite chemicals, which served as her residence and research laboratory.

Mother and son took a seat on the sofa in the living room, facing each other. Mountain air ruffled the curtains as it blew through the open window. The aroma of fresh pine filled the room. Attila leaned his gun against the armrest. Offering him a cup of cold tea, Mama Zany explained, "Attila, you were always my favorite chemical experiment. I named you just as you popped out. I named my mountain the same way I named you. Seize the moment! That has been my motto ever since you were born. Whether it is life springing from my womb, or the Peptide Chain bubbling up from the womb of God Herself, creation is the point. *Creation!* That's the key word: Create, create! Build, build! As soon as I moved here, I built the lunar laboratory of my dreams." She pointed to the back yard. "I built it behind the kitchen with my own money."

When Mama's peroration ended, Attila said, "I like this location. Your cabin is pretty, so restful." He paused to soak in the reflective atmosphere. "But, Mama, let me ask you a personal question: Why did you leave our house in New Jersey and move here without *telling* us? You've remained hidden so many years."

Mama Zany twisted her gray braid, rose to her full six-foot-four height, and, peering down at her son, responded, "My dear little starlight, as a woman of high standards, I had to get away from your father. At the time, his career was in chaos and his mental life a mess. Chemists such as myself, ever aiming for perfection, hate blemishes. Perfectionists hate slovenliness. Zoltan was a slob. His saving grace was his insistence on playing every violin note correctly. This desire helped us during our first year of marriage. I deeply appreciated and admired his love of correct notes. Unfortunately, he loved the notes more than me. He paid no attention and cared not a whit about my dreams of creating a lunar laboratory, chemistry, my intellectual and scientific development, or anything else *I* liked. When, during a chemistry experiment, I accidently blew up the garage, interrupting his scale practice, he felt his concert career threatened. He laid down his violin and insisted I give up my investigations. Well, I could live without him, but I certainly couldn't live without my work! So I moved out. As a loving mother, I didn't want to *disturb* my child. I didn't think you'd notice anyway. So when I moved out, I kept it secret because I didn't want to hurt you."

"But for two years?"

"You finally noticed!" Mama Zany raised her fist triumphantly in the air. "During this long hiding period, I realized I wanted recognition. I craved it, not only from Zoltan, but from my child! Yes, I wanted it from *you*. I also wanted recognition from the scientific community. I needed their confirmation of my work, and of myself as a scientist. I also wanted my community of chemists to love me. But they never did. I'm too tall."

"Height has nothing to do with love," Attila offered. He took a sip of the cold tea. "I recall that memorable moment, the day you finally called. What a surprise when the phone rang. We all thought you were dead."

Brunhilde shook her head, expressing affirmation in the Bulgarian style. "I remember the call. By then I had understood that recognition by He/She-Who-Knows was more important than acceptance by others." She sat down on a corner stool and leaned back against the wall. "As a little girl in Dusseldorf, rejection clouded my childhood. My parents' most popular word was 'Leave!' It hurt me so. One day, while performing a chemical experiment, I saw something new in the test tube. Recognition came in a flash of explosive light. The He/She said hello. A happy smile crossed my face as I cried, 'Ah, You love me!' That's why I became a chemist.

"How I remember that transforming day! Powerful neurotransmitters sparked my brain. Shining protons, crisp neutrons, beautiful amino acid chains, dazzling forms of protein accompanied by their protoplasmic friends, all ran helter-skelter through my mind-body connection. I became wiser. Love of Him/Her, accompanied by knowledge of the True Self, has little to do with recognition by others. These transient desires disappeared. I focused on the Great Chemist in the Sky. Ultimately, that's why I moved to Colorado."

Attila understood. "I like it, Ma."

A soothing quiet ensued. The lad gazed out the window at pine trees, mountains, verdant fields, streams, and rocks. Not a neighbor in sight. A look of concern crossed his face as he glanced at her. "Ever get lonely out here?"

"Never. Loneliness is not in my vocabulary. My lab creates a network of friends. Some stay here with me in chemical form; others visit on weekends. I also belong to the Science of Friends Society." Brunhilde pointed out the window to a distant mountain peak. "Our group meets at the foot of Mount Hieronymus on the first Friday of every month. There, stimulated by the cool breeze and fresh mountain air, we discuss the chemical underpinnings of friendship." Mama Zany raised her right index finger. "My son, I see people as amino acids. In my network of personal contacts, I link one friend to another. I play with their carboxl groups. Slowly, other amino acid friends move closer. Finally, when trust has been established, everyone bonds. I now have over a trillion-celled peptide friendships in my network."

Attila listened as a fresh idea emerged from the formerly vacant spaces of his mind. He watched it evolve, grow, shift, gradually changing form until finally, mature and fully grown, it burst, scattering seeds of expansion throughout his brain. Influenced by his mother's scientific methods and his father's metaphysical approach to violin performance and yeshiva-*sitz* armchair bottom placement, a weird combination of chemical doctor, linguistic priest, and philosophical rabbi of music, which called itself a "prabbi," had began to coalesce.

Mama Zany leaned toward him. She placed her ear above his heart. "I hear you thinking," she said. "Be careful. Watch out for the abyss."

"Thank you, Ma. I'm watching."

Attila stepped outside the cabin. He needed fresh air and time to think. Ambling through pine shadows, he sat on a rock, laid his gun to his side, considered the nature of growth, and pondered his future.

Would he develop a wider, even universal vision? Could he *become* a prabbi?

Three hours later he rose and headed back to Mama Zany for cup of tea.

5

MASHUGI

*I*N HIS SENIOR YEAR of college, Attila received a letter from the Israeli archaeologist, etymologist, linguist, scholar, and adventurer, Dr. Isaac "Cookie" Mashugi.

Here's how it happened: One of Dr. Zany's summer concert tours had included performances in Tel Aviv, Jerusalem, Haifa, and kibbutzim Beth Ha Hitchil and Jacov Makom ha Sevastopol. The morning before his Tel Aviv concert, the doctor had visited an archaeological site on the beach at Caesarea. There he'd chanced upon a group of archaeologists excavating Roman relics; they were joking loudly with one another in a strange tongue. The language he heard was not Hebrew, Russian, German, French, Arabic, or Hindi.

Piqued by his love of sounds musical and oral, and hoping some day to commission his friend the composer Ludwig von Batterhaven to write a *Concerto for Violin Linguistics*, Zany had moved closer. Finally, in frustration, he had asked the muscular, tanned, white-haired, mustached digger nearest him, "*Slicha*, Mr. Gentleman, do you speak any of the English tongue?"

Shouldering his shovel, the archaeologist had pushed back

his sun hat, brushed the dirt off his hands, and eyed Zany suspiciously. He'd picked up his knapsack, reached into it to pull out a falafel, taken a manly bite, swigged it down with water from his canteen, and asked, "Who wants to know?"

"So you *do* speak English."

"Everybody speaks English, even the termites."

"Good. Thank you. I'm a violinist. I've never heard such strange sounds. What language were you just speaking?

"Babylonian."

"*Really?*" Zany had been impressed. "Is there such a thing as Babylonian?"

"*B'vadai.* Of course."

"Is there much Babylonian spoken around here?"

"Only by us. We practice whenever we excavate archaeological sites. The Tower of Babel is my speciality." The archaeologist had reached into his pocket and pulled out a card. "I'm Dr. Isaac Mashugi, from Hebrew University. I like violinists. I play fiddle myself. I'm a Bach, Beethoven, Brahms, and Botticelli fan." He'd handed Zany the card. "If you want to play quartets or hear more Babylonian, give me a call. But decide quickly. Tomorrow I leave for Mt. Ararat."

Zany, squinting in the sun, had replied, "I was on a concert tour of Armenia three years ago. I saw the peaks of Ararat from my hotel window in Yerevan."

"That's nice."

". . .Mr. Mashugi, my son is a linguist. He's graduating this year with a degree in Etymology from Bustard University."

"Very good."

"Why are you going to Turkey?"

"Linguistic research. I'm looking for Noah's ark on Mt. Ararat. If I find it, I'll know what *really* happened at the Tower of Babel. But more important, I'm searching for linguistic information on the *first word ever spoken by mankind!* I have a feeling it's hidden in Noah's ark, perhaps among the animals."

"Aha!" Zany's mind had instantly leaped across the Atlantic to Attila in Colorado and the lad's passion for languages.

"Tell me, Mr. Mashugi. . ."

The archaeologist had relaxed, smiled, said, "My friends call me 'Cookie,'" and extended his hand. "You are now my friend. Call me Cookie."

"Okay, Mr. Cookie—"

"Just plain Cookie."

"Okay. . .Cookie. I have a son who is graduating from college. He has a passion for linguistics. Is there any chance that you, a lover of violin and scholarship, could help and guide him, become a kind of. . . mentor?"

"*Ayn beaya.* No problem. Some I ment, others I de-ment. I ment many. What kind of menting does he need?"

"Well, he needs to be put on the right path," Zany had explained. "Mostly life guidance. I'm sure he'd be a helpful addition for your Mt. Ararat adventure."

Mashugi had thought it over before asking, "Is he strong? Can he carry provisions?"

"Of course. Attila has built up his trapezoids, biceps, rhomboids, and rotators by carrying piles of books to his mountain cabin. He cut down trees to build an outhouse, hauled and chopped wood for the fireplace, decorated the cabin interior himself. He has strong hands from loading his AK-47, strong fingers from shooting it. We are of Hungarian origin with historic roots in Central Asia. That's why we named him after Attila the Hun. The lad's trigger finger is especially developed. He can protect you. He's an excellent shot."

"A gunner, eh? These archaeological trips are sometimes dangerous. We can always use more protection." Mashugi had glanced upward, then spat on the ground, uniting heaven and earth as he considered the future. "Here's what we'll do: Tell your son to write me. In the letter, have him detail, not only his qualifications for a Mt. Ararat linguistic adventure, but also his passions, interests, hopes, and dreams. Let him tell me what purpose and direction he wants his life to take. That sort of thing. Then I'll know what kind of kid he is. It will also set him thinking about his future."

"Excellent idea, Cookie. You're quite wise. I'll do exactly that." Zany had in turn extended his own hand. "Thank you, Mr. Cookie. I'll call my son right away.

Mashugi had nodded. "Very good.—*tov meod*, as we say in Hebrew!"

Zany had returned to the USA a month later. After unpacking and settling in, he'd polished his violin, dusted the books in his library, and paid Martha her monthly salary. Then he penned a Hungarian style, shamanistic-based, fiddle-tinged letter to his son at Bustard U.

Kedves Attila,

Soon you'll be graduating. Congratulations. Cso-dalatos! You'll depart from the safety and security of your intellectual nest. You'll enter the world at large, a place of pestilence, sickness, violence, thrills, studded with uncertainty, wild emotions, and directional mean-inglessness. It is a period of search and wandering for most youngsters—or middlesters, as may be the case with you. However, I have found a guru and mentor for you, one who can ease your pain of entry. I met him last month at an archaeological dig on my concert tour of Israel. A nagyon jo kind of guy! I had a short but fascinating talk with him. A linguist, researcher, adventurer, and teacher, I sense he is a master of men. Isaac Mashugi is his name. His friends call him 'Cookie.' This Mashugi would be wonderful to meet, study, and learn from. He is leading an upcoming archaeological and linguistic research expedition to Mt. Ararat in Turkey.

I spoke to him about your talents. He wants you to join him on this Ararat venture! However, before he can accept you into the program, he needs a letter about your interests, hopes, passions, and dreams—what you want your future direction in life to be. That sort of thing.

You'll find his address on the card enclosed is this envelope.

I know he'd be of great help during this adventurous stage of development.

With love,
Father Zany

Three weeks before graduation, Attila was nervously pacing his cabin. Uneasy about his future, confused about his goals, he pulled out his father's letter out of the desk drawer. Carefully, he read each line. The pace of his pacing increased.

Finally, he muttered to himself, "Time to write this Mashugi. He sounds crazy and wild enough. You never know where letters lead. Plus climbing Mount Ararat might straighten me out."

The next day he sat under a pine tree, booted up his computer, and composed the following:

Dear Dr. Mashugi,

(Or do you prefer Isaac? I've heard Israelis are informal.)

I am Attila Zany. My father, the violinist Zoltan Zany, says he met you near Caesarea a few months ago. Is this true? Did you like him?

My future goal: I want to become a prabbi. What exactly is that? For me, it unites science, metaphysics, biophysics, music, linguistics, philosophy, medicine, weaponry, defense, chemistry, history, and psychotherapy. I want to combine a universal vision with a job. My term for this as-yet-to-be-found occupation is prabbi.

In order to prepare this letter to you, I studied Hebrew. I have also thrown in some Aramaic, Phoenician, and Ugaritic, just to make sure. During my etymological studies, I discovered the Hebrew root "shemesh" means "to serve." Very poetic. I like it. The "shemesh" (sun) serves God's purpose.

I'm trying to find my "shemesh," my own purpose. So far it has eluded me. Are my wanderings part of a cosmic question? I sense Higher Forces speaking to me, suggesting my student days are over. Time to move on, do something else. But what? My dear Dr. Mashugi, that is my question.

Can you help?

Your (hopefully future) student,
Attila Zany

A month later, Attila drove to his post office to pick up his mail. The clerk in the booth handed him a pile of letters, magazines, advertisement, and postcards. Among them was a letter from Mashugi.

Startled, eyes wide in excitement and with trembling fingers, Atilla tore it open.

Dear Boy Attila,

The answer is yes. Yes, I want you to join my research expedition to Mt. Ararat!

Now the advice: Best for health, happiness, and a Mashugi life style is belief in progress, improvement, and eternal life.

Progress creates a positive attitude and helps cure unhappiness. Of course, since opposites attract, you need a descent into Hell, or Hades, as the Greeks call it, before progress can be made. Our trip to Mt. Ararat should provide that: a hell of a depression, which, as a good start, will be followed by an ascent on Jacob's ladder straight to Heaven.

Heaven leads to Hell, and vice versa.

Avoid dualism. Seek Oneness.

Now, my boy, the big question: Is there really a difference between Heaven and Hell?

Think about it. Give me your answer when I see you."

Mashugi

6

FATHER AND SON

DUE, ALAS, TO WHAT he lengthily described as "logistic and financial difficulties," Cookie Mashugi postponed his Turkish research venture to the following year.

Thus, after graduation, with linguistic degree in hand, trip to Ararat postponed, and no immediate job prospects other than his vague notion of prabbihood, Attila moved in with his father.

Living in the attic of Zany's quiet New Jersey home, the lad continued his etymological explorations. During this transition period, he studied for hours, sitting on a wooden stool, AK-47 at his side, language books piled high on a cedar table, the pages lit by a gooseneck lamp imported from Istanbul. As the weeks passed, he added Hittite, cuneiform writing practice, Akkadian, and bits of Ugaritic to his study ritual, as well as Turkish phrases, and exploration of Indo-European roots, Old English verbs, nouns, grammar, and, for relaxation at the end of each day, read passages from *Beowulf*.

Evenings, he descended from his monastic heights to practice target shooting in the back yard and to visit his father.

One day, he leaned his AK-47 next to Zany's armchair and asked, "Father, why do you keep scribbling in that book? Wouldn't your time be better spent studying military history, or learning the chemistry of bomb making?" He shot a few holes in Zany's notebook while waiting for an answer.

"Oh, stop it, Tommy," Zoltan hissed. "You're acting like Attila the Hun." He pushed the gun aside. ". . .As you know, your great-grandmother, the genealogist Zsuszi Kastoroszeg, told us that that famous bloodthirsty conqueror occupied something rather more substantial than a twig on our family tree. You were named after him. But that's no reason to belittle my journal."

Attila lowered his gun, lips sank into a frown, and asked, "Father, why do you always call me Tommy?"

Zany considered the question. "Tommy has always seemed to me to be a good nickname for daily life. Your mother and I knew such an appellation would get you through school without your fellow students mocking, laughing, or jeering at you. The name Attila is too powerful for the New Jersey educational system. Besides, our family believes in promoting disguises. Hidden names are a sign of strength. By hiding our identity, we become stronger. Now, Tommy, pick up your gun and listen to me."

Zany lifted his finger and rotated it in the air to promote circular thought. "Journal writing is a daily necessity. It clears the mind and helps preserve my sanity. The rich language in my garden of verbiage, especially when liberally sprinkled with Hungarian phrases and Finno-Ugric idioms, helps me dream and carries me to future places. In fact, through journal writing, I have even *met* your greatest of great-grandfathers, Attila the Hun himself."

Attila grabbed his weapon and riddled the ceiling with bullets of joy. Pride lit his face. "Meeting the Hun himself is no small feat! But, Papa, writing a journal still seems strange."

Dr. Zany disagreed. "Weapons may force others to acquiesce to your demands, but pens are powerful, too." He coughed, grabbed a handkerchief, and blew his nose. "I hardly slept last night." Reaching for his coffee cup, he took a meditative sip. "My mind is a confused mess today," he said, waving his son away. "Now leave me alone." He pulled out his pen, fixed his eyes on his journal, and unleashed a torrent of ink across the page.

An hour passed. Attila sat in his chair, waiting. Finally, Zany looked up. Relaxed and contented, his mandibular muscles forming themselves into a smile, he offered, "Writing down my thoughts brings such satisfaction. What about you, my son? What gives you pleasure?"

"Shooting."

"Anything else?"

"Marking linguistic books. I also like to throw dictionaries and grammars."

"I thought you *liked* languages."

"I do. But I express my joy of study *actively*. Books in flight give me pleasure. They intensify a Talmudic love of learning."

". . .You are a very strange child. What sort of family do you come from? Shooting, anger, love, hatred, joy. What kind of combustible emotional combination is *that* for a young lad?"

"Father, I go for high-octane joy. It creates a threat to my existence. I like that. When I feel joy, I want to vomit. Innards pop out, bile rises, esophagus contracts; I burp, cough, spit, and with power-pumping blasts, I expel suppressed bits of the devil. I see ancient faces and hear voices in my eyes. I'm afraid others may criticize me and ruin my fun."

"So," Dr. Zany suggested paternally from his armchair, "it is not joy you're afraid of, but the reaction of the *audience* to your joy! In their emptiness, you hear them shouting: 'How dare you have so much fun? How dare you enjoy yourself as long as others in the world still suffer?'"

He waited for his psychological insight sink in before adding wisely, "Fear is but one expression of the higher powers. Ills will pass. Through self-knowledge, your body heals itself."

". . .How?"

"Do you know about the curative power of endorphins."

"I've *heard* of them. Where do they fit in?"

"My son, as a Zany child, you were born with a fiery imagination. This gift gave you a landscape to work with: mountains, abysses, peaks, and pits. It gave you both freedom and terror. In order to harness these wild forces, your imagination created discipline, the creative road from fear to glory. Use it!"

Attila silently contemplated the dialectics of these opposites. After an hour, he rose, shouldered his AK-47, bowed to his father, and returned to the attic.

There among his books, sitting on his three-legged mahogany trinitarian thought-stool, he remained in a half-lotus for the next six hours. Deep in meditation, he visualized Finno-Ugric linguistic roots and Latin diacritical marks floating down his inner Nile. Biblical giants waved in the distance.

7

SEEDS

F INALLY! SEEDS IN MY garden," Zany purred, staring out the living room window. "How I love spring. Petite flowers of Zanyhood blossoming, trees flourishing, brooks flowing in many new directions. My flowers are my vegetable children. And now that my flesh-and-blood Attila is on his way, I can focus more attention on these fragrant beauties!" He observed the shining sun with cosmic pleasure.

The doorbell rang. Martha opened the front door to find St. James the Apostle standing in the doorway. The six-foot-eleven- inch business consultant was wearing his signature blue trousers, pin-striped shirt, and bow tie. "I'm here to plant hyperboles," he said.

Zany called his friend from his armchair. "My dear St. James, welcome to our spring festival. What took you so long? Flowers are popping. The garden is ready. Have you asked Loco Flores for her flowering maps? Wives know truths about gardening that mortal violinists fail to comprehend."

St. James winced. "Don't call Mad Mother Loco my wife. I'd never ask *her*. She knows nothing of the virtues of gardening." Zany yawned. Martha left the room as the apostle continued his tirade. "Why I married that woman, I'll never know. Since divorce is forbidden under the Metaphysical Gardening Statutes, Section 2—"

"Apostle," Zany snapped, "stop *whining!* I can't stand *hearing* your annual complaints. Can't you see the wisdom in her decision? Remember how she rescued you during your Crimean period, when the Tartar mustache roses got stuck in the lawn mower?"

"Stay out of my business, Zany!" St. James picked up the spring hoe lying beside Zany's armchair, swung it over his head, slammed it into the rug. He was about to dig a trench across the living room but stopped immediately. Winded, he leaned on the hoe and grunted, "Planting seeds is no easy task. Conquer the Kingdom of Speed and its dictator, Velocity. Wait for time to work its magic. . . . But you're right about one thing, Zany." The Apostle lifted the hoe to his shoulder. "By waiting so long to marry me, Mother Loco demonstrated that patience is the key to success. She sprinkled *legato* on my trees and flowers. The aquerosa vixen flower is my model for *patientia*. I'll admit, Mother Loco taught me the virtues of hardiness, resistence, stubbornness, and endurance. Slow planting, that's the way to go. In times of upheaval and tumult, only a hero dares to go slow. . . . You know, Zoltan, *you* could be that hero."

Zany snorted in disgust. "Oh, please. You give the same speech every spring. *Slow*, you say? *Agh!* I planted my garden that way for years! It was easy. *Too* easy! So I changed my style and went for speed. I planted at a lightning pace. I wanted to be the fastest seeder on the block, and make my deceased Mother Zany proud of me."

"You weren't mature enough to slow down."

Dr. Zany ran his double-stop violin concerto hand through his mane of white hair as he considered this wise assertion.

". . .Apostle, do you really think speed has caused my suffering?"

St. James calmed himself. Speaking in quiet, firm, philosophical tones, he explained, "There are so many causes of human suffering, it's hard to know which ones are yours. But certainly pain creates a blind, impassioned rush past the Gates of Understanding."

Outside, the spring sun was pouring on the sprouting grass. Zany's well-trained ear could hear flowers pushing their heads through the soil. St. James rose, exited through the kitchen door, pulled the gardening hose from its rack by the garage, and gently fingered its nozzle. Zany turned in his armchair to watch through the open window. "It's close to watering time," St. James called. "After I do your lawn and garden, I'll go home to practice. My goal is to play J. S. Bach in public."

"On the garden hose or the guitar?"

"This, of course." The Apostle turned on the hose. "Hosing practice has given me a love of wind instruments," he said as a spray of water, reflecting sunlight, fell on the garden soil. "I remember when dirt accumulated in my nose and I had to blow it out. I used a reverse breathing technique to suck up the leaves, grime, and bits of gravel. After the air passage was clear, I heard a half-whistling, half-humming, half-witted whirring sound. I loved it! The enormous musical potential of the hose became clear. I was hooked! Wind instruments and classical piping became my hobby, then my passion. Added to that, the sound of moving water turned Loco on! Another positive. My playing made her swoon!"

St. James returned to the living room, Zany reminisced, "I remember that Baroque period of your life. You refused to learn organ, clarinet, or any traditional instrument. Though you wanted to please your audience, you insisted on novelty, originality, and daring."

Dr. Zany pressed his hands together in a musical act of worship. "How splendid to be faithful to your vision while reaching for public adulation. I wish I still cared about such things."

"Some day you'll care again." The Apostle paused, hoping this prediction would take root. ". . .Zoltan, did you know we've named our performing group 'Gardeners Delight'? Our quartet of leaf blower, guitar, saxophone, and garden hose starts practicing this Sunday."

"Is performing with such a group worth the effort?"

"Good question. I've been exploring the floral ideas of Muhlhausen gardener Hammurabi von Tuttleberg, in his *Book of Babylonian Gardens: How to Build Paradise on Earth*, subtitled *A Teutonic Primer*. I believe my mature vision of garden music eloquence is in place. How to apply it is my current dilemma."

"I am also wondering about my next planting," said Zany.

ARE YOU JEWISH?

"ARE YOU JEWISH, DR. ZANY?"

"Of course, Martha. You know that from my writing."

"I have never seen you write, Dr. Zany." Martha rested a hand on her hip, and looked into the eyes of the good doctor. "Or perhaps I have," she reconsidered. "The nervous twitches, ecstatic arm and wrist movements you perform every morning: Is that *writing?*" Zany was about to answer when she added, "I thought they were involuntary muscular contractions before taking your medication."

"Now, now, Martha. The word is medi*tat*ion. You know I never take medication. I scribble higher thoughts on a pad every morning. Some may call it 'writing.' I call it synthesis and reflection. Holding my pen, carving words into a page, this 'writing,' *is* my form of meditation. I suppose some *might* consider it medication, since the process calms my mind. Writing medicates me into a meditative state."

"Dr. Zany, this is gibberish. I can't understand what you're saying! But, for *you,* such a lack of communication is a *wonderful* way to begin the day!" Martha smiled; mirth and incomprehensibility mixed in her eyes. "That is why I love working for you! Taking care of your worldly needs for so many years has been a daily adventure into the unknown."

"Thank you, Martha. You are a faithful servant, ministering to my body while I search for my soul. Mother Zany no longer visits me. You have become the closest thing to her presence."

Zany imagined his mother's celestial vibration. Grand Doctoress of the Maternal Mattress Erica von Fumbler, a.k.a, Sultana Ubersnatch, vaginal embodiment of a much faded Turkish Empire, now gazed down upon him. In dissolving-fusion dance, she transformed herself into a Teutonic knight, hiding her armor-clad form behind the northern facade of Malbork Castle in Poland.

This stellar vision vanished, leaving a sorrowful vacuum in Zany's mind.

The violinist faced the emptiness. "Aha," he sighed with illumination, "finally I understand. I've witnessed the disintegration of my old self. Down, down, it has rolled. Daily I sit in my armchair, descending further into the dark valley of desperation. Although the sun shines above me, its radiance brings no joy. I have everything and nothing simultaneously. In my rush to fill the demands from the old life, I have lost my spiritual center. Well, 'lost' may be too strong a word. 'Forgotten' is better.

"But I can feel that center rising again, kicking me like a baby in the womb. Yes, I need a new direction, a new mission and purpose. Determination, both conscious and unconscious, is my fulfillment technique. And I plan to sit in this armchair until I find it!"

The next day, Zany was reflecting upon his aching toe. "Imagination creates my physical failings. When they occur, I believe the worst. But suppose I imagined the best? What would happen?"

He paused to reflect on his reflections. "Maybe I *need* to worry.," he muttered.

"Dr. Zany, I am so *glad* that you worry," Martha called out happily from the kitchen as she cut up a squash for her French vegetable soup. "Anxiety unites you with the universe."

"Martha, you are so philosophical this morning."

"Yes. I am also right."

"'Philosophical' does not mean you are wrong."

"Well, whatever." She sliced some carrots. It was a clear day, and sunlight dappled the counter top. "This worry idea is more fascinating than doing the laundry. Dr. Zany, you are blessed with a wild, expansive imagination! It gives you the flexibility to worry about anything you like!"

"Anything. . . ."

"Yes. But secretly, I know you follow your own self-help program, the one you discovered seven years ago in Tashkent. Remember that Uzbekistan tour when you figured out how to handle stage fright? Your own invention, the *Fear Replacement Therapy Program,* worked! During that concert, in fact, you were so relaxed on stage, you fell asleep playing the Tchaikovsky *Violin Concerto.* Vibrations from your perform- ance were so powerful, the orchestra and audience fell asleep, too. When you heard your fans snoring, you woke up to finish the concerto. Next day you started writing about your new self- knowledge and created the pamphlet *Fear Replacement Ther- apy Rules,* which soon swept the music and psychotherapy worlds."

Zany's eyes closed as he recalled that concert tour of Central Asia. "Yes. It's coming back. You're right. I remember that, during the performance, the Uzbekistan police broke in to capture my wrong notes. I can still picture their black uniforms, clubs, and rifles. They searched under every seat and even frisked members of the concert audience!"

"Yes, *Doktor*. But now that your concert career is over, you have time to *focus* on your body falling apart. It's part of the rest period you recommended in your program!"

Zany mind drifted back in history. "It's hard to imagine I wrote such a curative book," he said, rubbing his aching quadriceps, gastrocnemius, and buttocks before moving up to his triceps and trapezius. "I'm tired of these sedentary cellular discomforts, suffering these persistent muscular pains. Isn't there a better way?"

"For you? I doubt it." Martha glanced upward as she considered the long slow period of Zany's transition plight. "Actually, I really don't know. We'll see what the Lord brings."

She dropped four tomatoes into boiling water, pulled them out, and began to remove the skins and seeds.

"Can't you save your religious opinions for the laundry?"

"Mein Doktor, the body is the clothing of the soul. It too needs cleansing. Though imagination is your essence, its flexibility may compromise your happiness."

While Dr. Zany thought about flexibility, Martha sauteed onions and garlic. "You mean enlarge my desires, expand my vision? If not, I'll focus only on aching body parts?"

"Exactly. . . ." She added three sprigs of thyme. "Ah, Dr. Zany, what a homey aroma!"

Zany sat in silence for the next few hours, considering his options. Martha mopped the kitchen floor where a fried fish had fallen.

Finally, he spoke. "Up to age eighty-three, Freud constantly revised his ideas. So should I. Vision enlargement is the way to go." A hint of enthusiasm entered his voice. "I'll revise my *Bumble Bee Concerto* and reexamine, restore, and improve my other compositions as well. I'll search for new meaning in the Bach *Chaconne*. New interpretations will flow."

Zany nodded as he agreed with himself. "Goodbye, nirvana, enlightenment, and yogic meditation. Inner peace is no longer my goal." Zany raised his hands, flailed the air in 4/4 time, and began conducting an imaginary Beethoven's *Pastoral Symphony*. "I prize the dynamic moments of restless imagination. I want battles of creativity shaping the rest of my life!"

Martha cleaned away the soup plates.

FIRE!

D R. ZANY WAS SITTING in his living room armchair, contemplating his future, when he happened to notice his house was burning down.

At first he paid little attention, thinking the flames would die away by themselves. But as wall boards heated up and ceiling burst into flame, he put aside his coffee, rose from his chair, turned to the open window, and shouted to Martha, who was raking leaves in the back yard, "Help!"

What had caused the conflagration? The long summer heat spell? Overcooked breakfast? A *Sitzensprintz* spark caused by over-inhabitation of his armchair? Or had it been his raging sore throat?

So hard to know the hidden causes of things.

Martha dropped her rake. "Call the *fire department!*" she cried. Attila came running down from the attic, AK-47 in hand, and started shooting into the flames.

Dr. Zany waved his arms in the air. This only served to fan the flames. Realizing the ineffectiveness of his approach, he turned to the phone and dialed a number scribbled on the wall:

(966)0446-9770-97753122-345797644.   The flames leapt higher. Martha raced up the back kitchen stairs, grabbed the phone from Zany's hand, and dialed the fire department.

"Treebeck Fire Department. Jones speaking. What can I do for you? Anything burning?"

"Our house is on fire."

"You've called the right number. What's your address?"

"422 Burdberry Avenue."

"I thought that one burned down last month. Well, never mind. We'll be right over."

Soon the wail of fire engine sirens could be heard up the street. Twenty firemen poured out of four fire trucks, carrying axes and a long hose. Entering through the front door, they sprayed the walls and living room floor. Suddenly, with a great crack, the kitchen ceiling fell. Pieces of the upstairs bathroom landed on the floor; then the bathtub crashed through, slamming into the kitchen table.

"Save your valuables!" the fireman shouted. "We don't know where this one will go or how long it will take."

Zany grabbed his armchair and pushed it through the living room window. It fell into the tulip bed with a thud.

They tried to evacuate Attila, who dodged them and raced through the dining room, shooting up Zany's den as he went.

Martha followed the doctor outside with an enormous tin of virgin olive oil and three pieces of fruit. Zany dragged his armchair to the front lawn. He sat down to watch smoke rising from the second floor windows. Martha and Attila sank onto the lawn next to him.

"I like fires," said Zany. "They were an important part of my youth. One of my early hobbies was burning down the forest behind our back yard."

Martha eyed him strangely. "It's true," she said as they watched the east wall of the kitchen collapse. "Fires can be soothing."

Zany meditated upon his childhood adventures as the flames rose higher; the burning house yielded many fruits for philosophical consideration.

"Fire reminds me of early traumas!" he said. "Ancient fears of abandonment! Ghosts of non-recognition are popping up everywhere."

Suddenly, a revelation seared his brain. "So that's why I've spent so many months in the house! By warming my chair, I was creating fires of lassitude. Tears of melancholy or sadness could not extinguish them. Now I know. Secretly, I was furious about my former life. No matter how hard I tried or how successful my concerts, I was constantly slapped down by non-recognition. And this slap down came from *me*. Even while the audience cheered, I was busy diminishing myself. I always knew the sad truth that, no matter how large my success, abandonment would follow. The sadness I felt during these months of armchair sitting is not due to old age or fear of death. Rather, it is memories of childhood traumas! Their reappearances destroy any chance of happiness or appreciation of my success."

The flames grew higher. Zany slapped his thigh with delight, rose, stood on the arm of his chair, and leaped into the air. In an instant, he was lying flat on the lawn, laughing, shouting, and singing as cries of freedom issued from his lips.

An hour later, firemen had hosed down the remains of his den. Zany considered the future. "I'll move slowly, carefully, return to old forms but with new wisdom. I'll start with. . . yes, the violin! I may even return to *concerts! Me!* Imagine that. But what about old fears? Memory lapses in public? Will I be brave enough to forget my music before thousands of adoring fans?"

As doubts invaded, Zany shook his head. Remembering the importance of blood supply in the brain, he turned himself upside down, stood on his head in a skillful *sirhasana,* the yoga pose he had learned from the kabbalistic yogina Balabusta Devananda after a fund-raising concert in the Himalayas. Pointing his toes south, north, then straight up towards heaven, he felt a rising awareness as currents of health-giving blood rushed to his temples. His face turned red. After eighteen minutes, a total Hebrew *chai,* he returned to his favorite resting position, the *savasana* or corpse pose.

Martha observed him. "Daring is good. You'll feel like a coward and failure if you don't try your best." She mopped the doctor's sweating brow with a handkerchief, then added with authority, "It's always better to give your best."

Zany sat up and straightened with attention. "You're right," he said. "To dare or not to dare—that is the question. Beneath daring lies *courage.* That's what Larry Columbus said before he discovered America. I'll say it, too!"

Martha agreed. "You must return to the concert stage, *mein Doktor.* If not that, to *some* public stage. Otherwise you will dry up inside and die."

"Yes. Some things are even worse than death. Now I realize that hiding in my closet is one of them."

"What about your stage fright? Isn't that why you stopped concertizing in the first place?"

"This fire has suggested a new attitude: giving concerts with different approach. Instead of running offstage when I forget a piece, I'll improvise and somehow slowly work my way back to the original piece."

Martha sympathized. Her eyes blinked in philosophic consent. "Forgetfulness will feed your imagination."

"Right. I'll conquer stage fright in the process."

"An added benefit." Triumphantly, Martha raised her voice and proclaimed, "Let creativity knock those little fukker fears right out of the box!"

"Yes! I'll do it! I won't let those little fukkers get away!"

Exhilarated, Zany took off his shirt, pants, and shoes, fell to the ground, and began a hundred joy-juice push-ups.

Just then St. James drove up in his Ford, the fully loaded fertilizer pick-up truck screeching to a halt by the curb. Balls of horse manure rolled out the back and onto the sidewalk. The Apostle had hoped to mow the lawn, and fertilize his rare Brazilian posthumoscarpial shrubs.

"What the hell is going *on* here?" he cried. Smoke was still rising into the sky.

Seeing the good doctor prone on the ground in his underwear, he called out, "Zoltan, are you all right?"

Attila ambled over, shot his AK-47 into the lawn one last time, and, facing his father, proclaimed: "Zanys believe in fight or flight!" Shouldering his gun, he ran past the firefighters into the burning house to save his last box of bullets.

One minute later, he exited the charred front door carrying nothing.

"Where did you pick up that piece of psychological wisdom?" Zany asked his son. The doctor still felt exhilarated by his exercises; he panted in happy mode.

"From shooting. It healed my back pain."

Zany shook his head. "You used to be such a nice, quiet boy, so placid and kind. But since you started with that gun three years ago, something has changed."

"You're right, Father. AK-47 has changed my life. I owe it all to you. Remember that Sunday afternoon when I rummaged through our garbage can and took out that soiled book? It was during our yard sale."

"What book was it?"

"*War Games and Back Pain.*"

"Ah, the one by Italian nutritionist Giovanni Sartorello?"

"That's it. The one you never read. Dr. Sartorello believed shooting others led to peace of mind, inner health, and physical fitness."

"Didn't they incarcerate him in Monticello Psychiatric? The schizophrenic patient section?"

"Yes. But realizing his genius, they allowed him to continue taking three shots a day from his window. Dr. Sartarello's book made me realize I suffered from TBP."

"What do those letters stand for?"

Attila had no idea.

10

SEARCH FOR DIRECTION

B UT AS HE SAT on the lawn, Zany was facing—despite the momentary emotional lift he had felt just after the fire—the emptiness of his future. He tried getting up, but a sudden vertigo forced him back to the ground. Finally, he rose, walked slowly to his front steps, and entered his home. He gazed in confusion at the embers of his former kitchen. "So many months of sitting. I never left the house. What will I do now?"

He returned to the lawn to find Attila sitting under a tree in lotus position, perusing a copy of Thucydides' *Peloponnesian Wars.* The etymological scholar had been thumbing through his notes on the conflict between Athens and Sparta. "'Athenian markets conquered the Aegean,'" he read aloud in his own translation from the ancient Greek.

"That's not in Thucydides," snapped Zany.

"It is in *my* translation!"

"After paying for all those classics courses at Bustard, you dare make it *up?* Shameful! What happened to your brain? That school messed up your medulla."

Attila's face reddened. He defended himself. "You didn't

waste your money, Papa! Classics are *right* for me. They helped get me into Harvard Medical School. Studying ancient Greek, Latin, Hebrew, Hittite, Akkadian, Syriac, Babylonian, Sumerian, and Ugaritic widened my social life—Radcliffe women wanted the Ugaritic type. They loved my original approach to translation." With filial concern, Attila looked into Zany's eyes. "Anyway, Father, you're doing it again. Avoiding, avoiding. Distracting yourself from facing your future."

"Well, with all your wasted education, what do you suggest?"

"Marketing."

"*Marketing?*"

"Yes. It will give new meaning and direction to your life. It's *good* to promote something."

"Attila, you're mad. Artists create art; marketers create markets. They are two separate entities. Artists cannot and *should* not sell. Never, never. Marketing is out. Besides, how could I possibly do both? Impossible. One life style cancels out the other."

"Father, this low-profile philosophy of yours has kept you prisoner in your pig pen long enough. Time to break down the walls and get out. You suffer from what Sartorello calls APS— Artist Pighead Syndrome. Marketing is *not* an annoying distraction—it can increase your visual powers." Emphasizing his point, Attila shot his gun into the air. "And bring dynamism to your life as well!"

"How do you know all this?"

"Shooting practice on the firing range has vastly increased my directional skills. So has my study of ancient Greek philosophy."

Zany considered this answer.

Then he began a long, thoughtful sit. Hours passed. The sun sank into the western sky; afternoon turned into evening. Chin in hand, he faced the darkness, pondering great questions in silent wonder.

The following morning, in the charred kitchen, Martha set up a breakfast table and pushed three metal chairs around it. Zany sat down, fondled his plate, tapped his knife and fork on a coffee cup in waltz rhythm, and asked his son, "Does this marketing really fit my personality?"

Attila snapped some bacon in pieces and arranged it on his fried egg sandwich. "Absolutely!" The lad bit into the sandwich and munched thoroughly before downing a glass of orange juice. Mouth loaded with food and stomach filling with authority, he continued, "Marketing, coupled with sales, will consolidate your connection to the public."

Zany remained silent. Martha set a boiled potato, cabbage, and a garlic clove on his plate. As she poured orange juice into his glass, he pushed back his chair, stumbled to his feet, and staggered around the kitchen. "Could this be where I'm heading?" he asked himself as chills of awe and wonder passed through him. The floor beneath his bare feet turned cold; he imagined ice beneath him as he suddenly remembered wearing torn fur mittens while playing a Bach gavotte during his concert tour of the Arctic. "If this *is* my new direction, what shall I market?"

At that moment, he saw his old self crumbling. Minutes passed as the demise continued. The sun peeked through the kitchen window; a robin chirped in the back yard. Rising imperceptibly, like a fog on the upland Scottish moors, the barest glimpse of a future Zany appeared. The chill diminished and disappeared; his frozen body softened to a warm glow. Clothed in mystery, he envisioned a life filled with potential and adventure. Spirit lasts forever. But was there really a connection between adventures Beyond and those in the here-and- now of the marketing world? He would see.

The great violinist knew, in any event, that his quiescent phase of house-sitting had come to a close; armchair existence was over.

What comes after an ending? A new beginning, of course! The Renaissance lay ahead. New life. *Resurrection.*

11

ZANY LEAVES THE HOUSE

WHAT A MORNING! A day for optimism filled with energy of repair: a *tikkun olam* morning. Shots of wild illumination, straight from Central Radiance Itself, pounded the sluggish spinal column of the somnambulant Zany. His eyelids fluttered. Incipient wakefulness stood within reach.

The house had been reassembled. Zany sat in his armchair.

But, that morning, sitting felt very different. From rear end to brain, a rare form of ancient enthusiasm had begun to percolate. Flowing up and down his spine, then moving into his throat, it made his vocal cords resonate with vigor; sparks coated his tongue. "Today is my day!" he proclaimed. "Hope and desire rising. This morning I'll get up, advance to the staircase, and, with luck, even make it to the second floor! Militating against my sleeping soul are subtle powers. I feel them stirring in my heart."

He shook his finger at the wall, rose from his armchair, took three steps forward, and looked boldly out the window. A cloudless sky mirrored the blue in his eyes; a blast of Eroica Beethovian energy jostled his being. Releasing a puff of velvet carbon dioxide, he smiled. "Ah, such satisfaction! I feel calm and peaceful. My innards are turning; a vague wildness simmers within. Today is rise-up day. I shall *walk*." Zany patted his chest. "Perhaps the fire helped after all. That pop, crackle, crunch, the pounding tympani of the kitchen ceiling collapsing, trumpets blaring, clashing cymbals of Wagnerian magnificence smashing the table to smithereens: In retrospect, how I loved it!" His eyes gleamed. "Yes! I'm ready! I want to meet my neighbors."

He opened his front door, inhaled a breath of fresh air, and descended the stone steps, and, with the delicacy of a ballet dancer, strode across the brick footpath and was soon standing on the sidewalk. Facing east, he squinted in expectation of harsh morning sunlight. Gazing in wonder at the Dutch colonial roof of his house, he turned, faced north, and ambled past the single-family homes to his right. "I want to meet my neighbors," he repeated.

He spied a large bearded man, with a black hat and black coat, walking his dog. Thinking of Moses leading the Children of Israel through New Jersey, Dr. Zany shuffled over.

"Good morning," he said. "Any commandments today?"

The man looked down at his leash and pointed to his dog. "Only for him."

"Are you not Moses?" Zany asked. "I think we met a while back."

"Forty years ago," the man answered. "Since then I've moved, had oral surgery, and become a linguist." He extended his hand. "Larry Linguini is the name."

As Zany shook the proffered hand, he asked, "Is your dog a linguist, too?"

"Yes. I named him Zeno, after that ancient Greek's paradox. He speaks Greek and can bark in Latin. But unfortunately, Indo-European roots have traumatized him. Six sessions with a canine therapist haven't helped a bit. The dog suffers from xenobarfia, an irrational fear of morpheme ingestion. Coupled with his genetic heritage of Lithuanian digestive enzymes, we believe this syndrome has created today's Baltic barfers in Vilna's suburbs."

The doctor listened in fascination. What interesting neighbors he had. Man and dog departed.

Zany crossed the street. A gray cloud filled with gloom and water formed in the sky. Suddenly it burst, pouring an inexplicable emptiness down upon him In seconds, his mind went from rich sonorities to blank pages. Sadness filled his puffy being. What was the matter? An hour before, he'd had everything. Now a vacuum of directional nothingness was filling his soul.

What could eradicate this foul mood?

Out of his back pocket, he pulled the cell phone that Martha had given him as a birthday present and punched in the numbers *641-222-6509 ^@)!#**. After three rings, he got Mother Zany's answering service, with Poe's raven reciting "Nevermore."

"Hello? Hello. . . Zoltan, is that you?" It was indeed Mother Zany's voice, celestial but distant. "How are you, my darling?"

"The gloom cloud rained on me," Zany whined.

"Don't worry, dear. I'll send the cleaning woman over."

"Why does this always happen?"

"Did you clean your room today?"

"I can't *stand* cleaning!"

"Take the ant way."

"What do you mean?"

"It's your father's expression. He's up here with me and says hello. Your Papa loved ants. He used ant psychology and work methods to build his nuclear waste company. He treated his employees like one big ant colony. Remember the motto he tacked on the office wall, 'An ant a day keeps the union away'?"

"Very smart. Pa actually believed that?"

"He certainly did. Collective psychology made him a wise man. That's how Zany Ant Works, Inc. got its name. Things get done when you follow insect ways: One grain of sand at a time—soon the anthill is built. Zoltan, go clean your room."

Zany got the message. Enough for one day. He crossed the street, returned home, and sat down again in his armchair.

12

PASTEL OF PEOPLE

THE FOLLOWING DAY, THE wind blew strong as Zany took another walk. Trees bent in his direction. He shuffled down the quiet streets surrounding his home.

A heavy woman dressed in slacks and ski boots pushed her baby carriage past him. Nodding a friendly hello, he asked, "Which way is heaven?"

The woman peered at him from beneath a green bonnet and, with a knowing look, leaned closer to Zany's ear and whispered in a low, conspiratorial tone, "Turn right on Maple. You'll see an ice cream store and Benny's Deli. Make a left, then catty-corner to your right. Zigzag sidewards, squat down near the fire hydrant on the corner of Syndrome Avenue, step off the curb and saunter to the left. You should see Heaven just ahead of you."

"Thanks for your time and very exact directions," said Zany. He bent to kiss the baby, but the woman gave him a sharp kick in the shin.

As he scurried off, he muttered, "I spoke to that woman for less than a minute. Yet after I connected with her and she with me, I felt energized and awakened!" Wincing from shin pain but excited as well, he concluded, "Talking with others, dealing and working with them, even giving concerts, *energizes me!*"

The kick in the shin reminded him of his concert career and the boos and hisses from irate audiences. Even then, this form of *rejection* had energized him! He also remembered standing ovations from his fans. "We connected across the world," he muttered to himself and the adjacent tree. "Positive or negative didn't matter that much. I shared their power. What a wondrous thing. Now I understand what St. James meant when he said, 'Travel inward, down and deeper. Finally you reach the sacred interior spot of darkness. That's where you'll find your sun. Once you find your sun, it will shine on everyone and everything around you.'"

Zany considered these words. "The nature of light is to shine. My job is to find the light. The rest will take care of itself."

He continued down the streets, past pleasant suburban homes; dappled light fell on their lawns. His pace picked up when he crossed busy Maple Street, eyeing the changing traffic light with caution. Lost in his own thoughts and reveries, he hardly noticed the noisy teenagers hanging out in front of Benny's Deli, taunting each other, laughing, and shouting strange words in Turkish and Armenian. He treaded on for many blocks.

A car jammed on the brakes and screeched turning the corner at Synod Avenue. A man in a dark suit was walking his dog, who stopped to sniff a fire hydrant.

All at once, a magical light exploded above Zany. Stunned, he looked first heavenward. Patches of blue sky broke through the clouds. He turned his vision inward. Near his heart, above the right ventricle, he saw hundreds of people dancing and shouting with joy in the rain. Large and small, fat and thin, black and white, red and brown, pink and purple, babbling in a hundred languages.

Moments later, they merged into a rainbow and collectively rose in a pillar of fire before disappearing behind a cumulus cloud. A pastel of leaders appeared near the sun. Shining and brilliant, with hands raised, they blessed the pastel of people and motioned them to follow uphill towards an imaginary summit. Smiles, laughter, tumbling, and high-pitched giggles accompanied their naked progress.

It was a *Zany* vision.

Yes!

First, he denied it. Confused and irritated, he told himself that, like pain, the pastel of people must be imaginary, a mental trick.

But life takes place in the mind. His imagination had created his story. Why diminish the miracle? He looked up again; an arc of sky slowly opened. Blue sky. Shining sun. A new world emerged.

Dizzy and faint, Zany fell to the ground.

Hours later, the doctor had still not come home. Martha called the police. Sirens wailed. They found the violinist sleeping under a tree in a park. They drove him home, and, aided by Martha, helped him up the stairs, across the living room, and into his armchair.

There, in a seated position, he slept for two days.

Saturday morning he awoke. Birds were chirping outside his window. He blinked, yawned, and listened to their familiar melody. Were these avian missionaries singing the first measures of the Mendelssohn violin concerto?

"Birds know their business," he said. "And I know why. They do what I have *not* been doing over this past, disintegrating year. They *follow their discipline!* When the Master Musician created them, He gave them orders, told them what to do. Aviologists call it 'instinct.' I call it *discipline*. When the Master created me, He gave me orders, too." Raising his thin right arm, weakened from months of disuse, Zany brought his palm down hard on his thigh, slapped his face, smashed his left shoulder, beat his neck, breast, chest, and heart before kicking his chair five times. He pushed himself up, lifted his eyes towards the ceiling, and, gazing heavenward, shouted his Freedom Proclamation: "I'm sick of armchair life! Watch out, condiments. I'm returning to my commandments. Discipline, here I come!"

He leaped out of his armchair, raced across the living room rug straight to his violin case. He snapped it open, grabbed the fiddle, stuck it under his chin, lifted his bow, and began the Brahms violin concerto. After a few measures, his unpracticed fingers began to ache. "Aha, I forgot to warm up. Finger heat, body heat, mental focus. Fifteen minutes of warm-up scales and arpeggios are absolutely essential. Yes!"

13

BUSINESS

D R. ZANY ROSE FROM his armchair. Pride filled his legs. He scratched his neck, straightened his tie, and buttoned his shirt. With powerful strides, he crossed the living room, pulled open his front door, and shouted to his neighbors and all the world to hear, "My vacation begins today!"

He descended the front stairs and began a slow jog down the street. Puffing past Apple Lane and the fancy extension built by his neighbor, Morris Appleblaster, he wondered, Why did I say that? What vacation am I talking about? Perhaps it means I'm out of my armchair and out of the house for good. Yes! Trotting down the road of life, planning my next direction. I didn't expect this, but here it is. New attitude time. I need a shift in volume, a radical change of substance, a different style, a meta-formation and transmorphosis from my previous existence. Yes, *ken, igen, oui, ja, si, ne, da*, I'll say it in every language I know! In the future, let me live in *vacation mode!* Stooping to lace up his shoe, he reflected further on one knee as the scent of fresh laundry wafted towards him from the Waffenblathers' brick house to his right. "I'm not sure what 'vacation' means yet, but I sure like the sound."

He ran for an hour. Strengthened by the flow of endorphins, his unconscious mind created new pathways in the verdant fields of his conscious mind.

He reached his home, panting and breathless. Staggering through the front door and into the hallway, he shouted, "Vacation, vacation!"

Attila was sitting on the living room sofa, waiting for him. "So do I," he replied as he slid bullets into the magazine of his pistol. The linguist then lay his copy of Plato's *Republic* on the table and shot three holes in it.

Martha carried a half-baked yam across the floor. "I agree, Doctor."

"Agree with what?"

"A good vacation will relieve your bad back."

"I don't have a bad back."

"See? It's working already." Martha cut into the yam with a fork and said, "Attila and I both think you need a vacation."

A few days later, the town firemen returned for a final house check. They hosed down the basement, axed an attic door, read phrases from Zany's extensive library of ancient and modern history, and checked for any embers remaining from the conflagration. Task completed, they dragged the last of their equipment out of the house. Captain Harry Higgly turned to Zany. "Everything's safe now," he said. "We reported the fallen ceiling to the building department last Monday. They know about the collapsed south wall, burnt back porch, and smoke damage in the living room. But now, things look pretty good." Higgly signaled his fire inspector. "Leave the water damage in the basement for tomorrow. Let's go." The men climbed into a waiting fire truck and drove off.

St. James arrived just as the inspector and his assistant were leaving. "Thank God *that* horror is over," he said.

"It's not over until I solve *my* problem," said Dr. Zany.

"That could take years," said Attila.

"*Whatever* it takes!" snapped Zany.

"I can steer your gardening adventures and even plant some tulips along the way," offered St. James helpfully.

"We'll deal with that later," said Martha. "For now, let's bring our chairs outside. This spring weather is so balmy. We can sit outside for hours. . .even days."

"How about years?" Attila suggested.

St. James echoed Zany: "Whatever it takes."

Martha and the Apostle gathered lawn equipment from the garage, including chairs, a plastic table, and blankets.

Martha carried out a tray of fruit juice and bagels. St. James sat down on a lawn chair, nibbled a bagel, and took a sip of pomegranate juice from his glass. "Did I hear you guys talking about a vacation? It's good to take time off. Zoltan, this is part of your old philosophy."

"How's that?" Zany asked.

"For years you *played* the violin and gave concerts. Now this 'play' agenda has advanced to encompass, not only violin, but all of *life!* The broad, innocent vision of life as a playpen."

He chewed thoughtfully, took another sip of juice, and lifted a finger in the air. "You're at the resolution point. A new stage. Resolving conflicts. The question: How to combine life of an artist with. . .what?"

"Businessman!" Attila exclaimed.

"*Businessman? Me!* Attila, where are your brains? We

went *through* this once. You've been shooting too much. You know how I hate business. That's why the Mammoth Agency and Larry Pewterhoff have handled all my bookings for years. I never touch the gory aspects. Business is for capitalists, entrepreneurs, and wild men. Not me. I'm an artist!"

"You *were* an artist," said Attila. "You've been sitting at home for over a year. Who knows what you are now?"

St. James demurred. "Once an artist, always an artist. However, you may need to express your art in a different *way*."

Zany perked up, fixed his searching eyes on the Apostle, and exclaimed, "Tell me more."

"Zoltan, it's quite simple. When I gave up my life as a piccolo soloist many years ago, I moved into my father's pickle business. He fired me when I began making piccolos out of pickles. But I persevered. After leaving his factory, I began starting other businesses. Finally, after many trials and years of experimentation, I discovered gardening. I've remained faithful to its calling ever since."

Martha listened with approval. "My Apostle," she said, laying an approving hand on his shoulder. "Your consistency is your strength."

St. James turned toward her and nodded in acknowledgment. "During all this time, my artistic soul has never changed," he went on, "but my methods have. I've used a variety of tools to express my dreams and visionary side. Presently, I paint upon a wider canvas with a variety of brushes. Zoltan, your new business painting ought to express variety. In fact, I'd suggest creating a 'pastel of people.'"

Stunned by the Apostle's insight—he had not mentioned his vision to a soul—Zany could only grunt in a gravelly voice, "Nice metaphor."

St. James rose, stretching his frame the full distance to emphasize his point. "A *meaningful* metaphor. Pleasant and playful, too. Think of violin notes as people. Put them together, and you've got a symphony. As an entrepreneur, you could call it a *business sonata*. When I worked for my father, I composed a thing I called 'Sonata for Piccolo and People.' The title itself went through several transformations. First came 'Sonata for Piccolo People,' followed by 'Piccolo People Sonata.' Then came 'Sonata for Pickles and People.' Finally, I settled on 'Sonata for Pickled People.' A winning title! It still brings me royalties. In a stroke of marketing genius, I made even more money selling it to the United Undertakers Association of America. As you know, over the years, it has become a national anthem for the posthumously challenged."

Zany's eyes shone with delight. The violinist recognized the promotional savvy of his business mentor. "I remember that sonata. What sonorities!" The doctor envisioned dollars floating and flying into the Apostle's coffers. "You made so much money on it! Indeed, it proved you are a marketing virtuoso." Zany retreated into himself; his eyes turned inward in a self-searching effort. "Anyhow, back to me: Okay, I'll move to the Land of Infinite Vacation. But I've never taken a true vacation. I don't even know what it *is*. Let me ask you: *Can business be a vacation?*"

"A wise question, Zoltan. Easy to answer, but hard to put into practice." St. James sat down, fondled his fruit juice cup and bagel, glanced at a passing cloud for its water of inspiration. "Living your life as a vacation is an art form. It is *the* true art form. Many years ago, I climbed Mt. Sinai. I remember standing at the peak. As dawn broke, a brilliant sun rose in the sky. Suddenly, I felt a chill of wonder on my shoulder.

I had a visitor. The Lord Himself had swooped down in the form of a pigeon. Flapping his wings, He pecked at my neck and placed an invisible seed in my ear. I could feel the pigeon sprinkle on my neck. Some of my secular friends said nasty things about the bird, but I *knew* it was some kind of religious calling. The seed hit my cochlear nerve before sailing down my semi-circular canals, and finally sprouted between my trapezius and levator scapula muscles. Suddenly, a flash of lighting, a roll of thunder, and a commandment stone appeared before me with my future direction written in Hebrew letters. The pigeon immediately translated the text for me. I heard the Lord transform my name to "Apostle." He demanded I heal the world by committing myself to mitzvah through business."

Raising his voice in excitement, Attila broke in, "I had a similar meeting! He descended in the form of an ant. With a totally different message."

Reverence for the higher forces flooded the mind and soul of St. James. He bowed his head with respect. A long moment of silence ensued. "Yes, of course," he said in soft, humble tone. "Each soul is unique. Each one receives a different message. We all have a special purpose to fulfill in both this life and the next. After my meeting, I changed my entire name from Jan Bifurcatsky Choplesz to St. James the Apostle."

Zany sat back in his chair. "I remember how you complained about that name in grammar school," he recalled, taking another bite from his bagel. "Kids always mispronounced it. Who knew Polish? Even after you insisted on correct pronunciation, patiently explaining us how to make a soft guttural 'ch' from the back of your throat, our third-grade teacher, Mrs. Bender, still threw you out of the class for spitting. But Polish is hard. Even I, a musician, couldn't pronounce it. That's why I called you Hopeless for so many years."

The Apostle's eyes curled back as his mind unveiled pictures from his elementary school days in P.S. 7, nicknamed Riverdale School for Delinquents. "Zoltan, you were my only friend then. But I'm happy to say that now, with my wealth from royalties, I have many more."

"How much do you pay for each friend?"

"I use a straight-line method to assess their true value. Friends who visit are worth more than those who don't. But as I grow older, I need more time for myself, more peace and quiet. So I've reversed the valuation. Now friends who *don't* visit get paid the most."

"A wise decision. In our later years, we need more days of solitude for reflection."

"Precisely."

"St. James, my Apostle, I find a message in your lifestyle. But my question remains: Are there entrepreneurial and business benefits it can bring me? What about *music?*"

"There you go."

"But I've gone the concert route. What else could I *do?*"

"Zoltan, you're asking the right questions! For answers, consult the bush in your back yard."

"It burned in the fire."

"All the better! Is it still burning?" St. James did not wait for an answer, but ploughed on with his teaching. "God spoke to Moses through a burning bush. I'm sure He'll speak to you, too. Ask Him if business can be a vacation. But first ask yourself: What *is* a vacation? How does one guard against VDS—vacation disorder syndrome?"

Zany considered his friend's wise but enigmatic words. Unconscious reflexes set in: He tapped the rhythm of Vivaldi's violin concert in A minor with his foot; sweat formed under his armpits and rose to his mind, causing a bead of perspiration to appear on his forehead. With a nervous twitch, he pulled the Kalosca-embroidered Hungarian handkerchief from his pocket and wiped his brow. Dealing with his life's direction and the higher forces guiding it was making him uncomfortable. "Aren't hard work and vacation opposites?" he asked. "Wouldn't combining them be an oxymoron?"

"Indeed it would," St. James emphasized. "But I *believe* in the oxymoronic life! Its basic tenet is: The harder you work, the greater the vacation! It's all explained in *Autobiography of an Oxymoron: Self-Fulfillment through the Oxymoronic Life*, by Basil Bladdersworth. Basil was the son of an esteemed Hittite scholar/vacation expert, the scholarly Babar Bubbysnatcher, of Hiphugger, Nebraska."

Zany looked up. "I've been to Hiphugger, but I never heard of Bubbysnatcher."

"Not many have. He avoided casual contact. Nevertheless, Zoltan, one *needs* a broad view to cover all angles. Just as biblical exegesis has four levels of interpretation, so does vacation mode. First comes the simple level, dealing with what, where, how, and when you take a vacation. Caribbean in January, a summer in Iceland, stay home for the weekend: Those would be choices at the simple, or 'explicit' level. Next comes vacation 'hints.' What does your vacation *imply?* Is there a hidden, deeper meaning—a hint, wink, Hebrew *remez*, an implicit suggestion that better things will come? Third is the *interpretive* or metaphorical level: What does your vacation mean *personally?* Here you start visualizing it vacation as an adventure of the soul. It becomes an exploration of the meaning of life. Finally, on the fourth, most subtle of levels, you look into vacation's *mystical* aspects. What is its purpose in the greater scheme of things? How does vacation relate to the Higher Forces? Did the Big Boss order it for you? Is He part of your vacation? Is He in on it with you? Who *really* is that person in a bathing suit, lying next to you in the sun? Do they have a purpose beyond just lying there? Are they angels conveying important messages to you in vacation form?

St. James observed Zany's jaw slowly dropping as the violinist listened with awe and full attention. He paused, to let his message resonate. A bird flew past the half-open window; rays of sunlight dripped through the screen. "Zoltan," the Apostle continued, "combining business with relaxation is a high art form. It's not easy. But for you, it is possible."

"I shall contemplate—"

"Indeed, Zoltan, you must do it. For physical and mental health. You need a cause to lift, rouse, and expel you from your sedentary armchair existence, to energize you again in a new fight for survival. What better cause than creating your own business, one that becomes a total expression of yourself? After sitting around with bowels and soul cooking for over a year, I know you're ready to move on."

An eerie stillness descended upon Zany. He sat still for fifteen minutes as these new ideas washed over his being, seeping into his formerly sleeping, vacant, but presently awakened mind. Finally, he said, "Apostle, thank you. You bring me hope. These ideas are truly different. In fact, they remind me of the violinist Henry the Barbarian. A great virtuoso! When I heard him play Sarasate's *Zigeunerweisin*, I couldn't sleep for days. What *pizzicato*, speed, and vibrancy! At that time, I couldn't imagine why he gave it all up to go into the meat packing business. Now he performs the violin masterpieces of Brahms, and Vivaldi only in freezers, where cows listen hanging from their hooks. Last time I visited him, Henry seemed happy. Although he didn't say much, just a moo or two."

"A good example to follow," said St. James. "Here's an even better idea. You've concertized for years, you know hundreds of musicians—some of the bests, plus agents, managers, many others in the music industry."

"Yes?"

"They need work."

"Yes. . . ."

"Why not provide it? Start a music agency. Promote these virtuosos. Most of them need the business. They lie around the house all day waiting for the phone to ring."

"Well, I don't know—"

"You're a good salesman, Zoltan. I've seen you work the room. If you can get an audience to listen with rapt attention to a Bruch violin concerto, you can get them to do just about anything. Representing and promoting concert artists would be a boon to humanity. . .*and* fill your coffers."

"You think I could make *money* at it?"

"Of course. The world needs art. You can sell it! In the meantime, keep practicing your violin. Give a concert every year or so. It will increase your sales and give you pleasure."

"Hmmm. . ."

St. James pushed further: "Although, as a concert manager and agent, you'll have lots of headaches, you'll also have lots of fun. It is the perfect venue for a working vacation."

"An agency, eh? . . . Me? Well, I don't know. . . . Perhaps. . .I might. . .but—I like . . . no. . . .Yes, it's. . . hard to. . .okay, I—"

"You don't have to decide today. Think about it. Wait until your house cools down."

\

14

TRANSFORMATION
BATHROOM CONFERENCE

S ELF-DESTRUCTION CAN BE VERY satisfying," said Dr. Zany. So
began his bi-monthly upstairs bathroom conference, organized to further explore new directions in his life.

Zany sat soaking in his sea-salt bubble bath.

Martha looked at the good doctor hidden beneath a mound
of bath bubbles. "Indeed," she said, "Jason Reich Hegel, greatest
of Friedrich Hegel's grandsons, would have agreed with you."

St. James was sitting with his legs crossed astride the closed
commode. "You knew him?" he asked.

"Of course. We met in the basement of Dusseldorf's Wallet
Store."

"Strange name," said St. James, a puzzled look on his face.
"What kind of place was that?"

"All the town pickpockets met in the Wallet Store. Most
were gypsies from Romania. They gathered there to share and
exchange stolen wallets."

Attila stroked his chin thoughtfully. "Attitudes toward petty
theft were hardly considered by the ancient Greek philoso-

phers," he remarked from his wicker chair in the corner. "The fifth-century Ionian philosopher Dionysus Diklopodes did explore kleptomania. He was part of an ancient think tank working out a new vision of atomic theory. Contrary to Thales, who believed all things, including people, were made from atoms, Dizzy Diklopodes thought atoms were made of people."

"How informative," said Martha. "Did you learn that in college?" She rose to sponge off part of the sink. "What kind of name is Diklopodes?"

"Greek, of course."

"Do you know what it means?"

"'Double thief,' I believe. Lots of citizens had second names in the fifth century B.C. By the way, Martha, what is *your* second name?"

What *was* Martha's second name? Due to certain secretly possessive aspects of Zany's character, nothing about his homemaker had ever been revealed to family or friends.

However, Zany himself, before hiring her, had done extensive research. According to the Munich historian Dumbford Plato, Martha had many second names, but, due to an inherited family disease, remembered none of them. Whenever family members thought about their history, a virus of forgetfulness, the so- called *lethe porcupineus*, attacked their blood stream, entering the brain through the longitudinal right canister vein, and caused immediate memory evaporation.

Martha's family tree thus consisted of lost souls sliding helter skelter up and down its memory trunk. During her rebellious youth, much of which she had spent hiking and yodeling in the Tyrolean Alps, Martha had made a herculean effort to recall her family name, but to date only the first syllable had emerged.

Now, having finished sponging off the bathroom sink, she sat on the bathtub rim to offer Dr. Zany his morning breakfast. Lifting a forkful of torched power pasta from a porcelain dish to within an inch of his waiting lips, she added: "Munch these morsels of twig-spaghetti. Their carbohydrates will nourish your memory and brain power."

Dr. Zany leaned forward and opened his mouth wider. "Very tasty, Martha. I feel a full direction coming on."

"A bathtub sitter can do that," said St. James. "It's the Greek way."

"*Greek?*" Attila asked. "What do you know about Greece? Do you have any notion of Byzantine fire, Platonic dialogues, Hades, Hellenic power?"

"Oh, why did your father ever bother sending you to college?" St. James snapped.

"Lost souls flourish in college," Martha offered in defense.

"Stop arguing," Zany commanded. "These conferences are not about you, but about *me!* I am the one who is lost."

He reached for the washcloth and soap. "*Ow!*" he yelled, "My back!" His face scrunched in pain. "Spasm, spasm!" He sank back against the wall of the tub. "Damn this back! It keeps going out. Why can't I be normal like everyone else? My damn body is attacking me."

"It's tension," said Attila. "You've been lost too long. Going sideward, backward, overland and underland, has just been too much for you. The house burning down was a finale. The Zany brain can't take it anymore. Your nerves are affected. . .and *in*fected. No wonder your back keeps going out."

"I have back problems, too," said St. James calmly. "But I know how to handle them."

Zany looked hopefully at his business mentor. "What do you do?"

"My method is so simple that only a fool can do it."

"I'm ready," said the doctor.

"When my back goes out, I *focus* on the pain," St. James explained. "Then, and here's the key: *I try to make it worse.*"

"*Worse?*"

"Yes. It works every time."

"Are you insane? I want to make it better, not worse."

"Hard to believe my method is so good. But it is. I first tried it five years ago when I fell down the stairs trying to paint the ceiling. I rubbed my back, put ointment on, rested, took pain killers. . .nothing worked. When I went back to painting three months later, I fell off a ladder. Two days later I fell down the stairs three times in a row. By then, I couldn't avoid it anymore. My back was killing me. I *had to focus* on it. Suddenly, for no apparent reason, my pain started dissolving. The more I focused, the more it dissolved. After ten focused minutes, it disappeared completely! I fell down the stairs only once after that.

"Now, whenever my back hurts, I put my total focus on it and try to make it worse. My back gets better every time."

Zany had stopped soaping himself. A glint of hope appeared in his eyes. Nevertheless, he looked skeptically at the Apostle. "I've been to many doctors. None have ever counseled such a method."

"What can you lose?"

Zany felt desperate. Over the years, pills, massages, hot baths—nothing had worked.

"Try it, Pa," Attila urged. "The worst that could happen is nothing."

"Nothing is better than what you have now," added Martha.

Zany closed his eyes. He gathered all his creative power-sand forced them through his spinal column. The energies flowed directly into his coccyx.

Sure enough, the pain in his lower back got worse. Two minutes and thirteen seconds went by. "It hasn't changed at all," he said.

"Keep trying," said St. James.

Four more minutes passed.

"Damn, it's getting better!"

15

THE FUN CHAI

SOAP BUBBLES ROSE FROM Zany's bathtub as the conference continued. St. James, sitting still on the edge of the toilet seat, leaned toward the soap dish and looked straight into Zany's eyes.

"Business," he explained, "is play with money attached. Play in action. Fun stands at its foundation."

Zany swabbed soap under his arm, rubbed vigorously, and considered this notion. "I like it," he said. "Your business philosophy confirms my view."

The violinist again lowered his torso into the warm water. He scratched his head, massaging his scalp, stimulating thousands of brain cells, before directed his gaze towards St. James. "But my Apostle, here is a most important question: What about art?"

"Art is a business. Business is an art." St. James rested a firm fatherly hand on Zany's knee. "*Fun* is the place where business and art meet."

"Really?"

"Yes. It's a dialectical dance. As a couple, they join together in a synthesis of Hegelian fusion. This is the opposite of Marxian con-fusion. Zoltan, your love for life come from the arts, music, books, study, and your most recent exploration into the intellectual life of turtles. However, my love of life comes from and through *business*. In business, I begin by setting huge, apparently unachievable goals for myself. It's a challenge to try to fulfill them. If by chance, I succeed, as often I do, then it is my *greatest* pleasure to try going *beyond* them!"

The conference moved through many phases, conversations, dialogues, monologues. Finally, when fatigue set in, one by one, first Attila, then Martha, followed by St. James, rose, said goodbye, and left. Zany remained alone in his tub. The water, turning colder, energized him. He rose from his bathtub, toweled off, sat down on the toilet seat, and, for the next three hours, lost himself in contemplation and inner exploration. Notions of goals, growth, business, music, and self-development flitted through his mind. "If only I could figure out which self is me," he complained to the walls in general and toilet seat in particular.

"You like all of them," answered the seat.

"Perhaps," Zany answered. "But truth is, until this conference began, I always disdained business. On top of that, I detested the Apostle's business model.

"Nevertheless, the warm water, my stage of life, being surrounded by smart and caring friends. . .somehow this meeting has changed me. I'm starting to look at things differently. Maybe I've seen business in a narrow-minded way. If it took seventy years for the Soviet Union to fall, maybe it takes just as many years for my attitudes to fall. Perhaps they already have. *If* they've fallen, am I ready to recognize their collapse?"

Zany pondered this as he flushed the toilet. Sounds of swirling water coupled with the empty bathtub alerted him to the power of a vacuum. Nature abhors a vacuum. An empty mind creates a mysterious power, an unknown force yearning for fulfillment. His own emptied mind was ready for something new, vital, and challenging to rush in. "Fill me with good stuff!" he shouted. "Create a new mind set! Shall I consider giving up my old, worn-out attitude towards art and replacing it with business? "

St. James poked his head back into the bathroom. Evidently, he had just stepped outside for a breath of dry air. "Remember, fun, adventure, and creativity," he said. "Cement those forms together! It's the Camino de Santiago, Le Voie de St. Jacques, the St. James Way!"

"Thank you, Apostle, for reminding me again. As I review my past, I realize I may have had your perspective all along. I just never recognized it. After all, look at my leadership of the Boys against the Girls club in second grade in Barnfarht School. Or how, at the age of nineteen, I left my comfortable home with Mama and Papa Zany to spend a year in France. Or the courageous concert touring life I led. These all point to fun, adventure, and creativity. But I didn't put them in St. James' business terms. I didn't recognize them. Perhaps unconsciously I even *refused to recognize* them!"

Zany considered his past. His concept of an artist had been that of a soloist who created in his room and remained oblivious, even disdainful, of the outside world and the lowly denizens inhabiting it. He considered businessman strident, uncaring, clumsy oafs who strode squarely through the world, bashing customers as they egotistically manipulated them solely to increase profits. Hating businessmen was a family axiom. What leftist, anti-capitalist artist could admire those paragons of greed, selfishness, thoughtlessness, and evil?

Then a paradoxical thought rose in Zany's mind. He chuckled. How ironic if, hidden in the deepest recesses of his mind, had always lurked a secret capitalist, a *closet businessman!*

He also like the Apostle's idea of inventing huge, apparently unachievable goals.

He put on his bathrobe, slipped into his slippers, and stumbled out of the bathroom, wondering. What would life be like beyond the toilet?

He knew his brittle, crusty, ancient armchair life had died. He could hear its funeral song offered by crows sitting on a branch of the maple tree outside. Spring was in the air and in his step. Rebirth. Time to plough mental pathways, sprinkle fresh seed, grow fresh and future flowers, start a new garden.

He stood before his favorite Van Goggle painting of swirling flowers surrounded by blue sky and drenched in sunlight.

He scratched his chin. "How shall I unite business and art? Well, I'll figure it out. I'm warming up for my next adventure." He strolled around his living room. "A crossroad. My mind is divided. I'm in a perfect place for a new beginning.

16

BUSINESS STRATEGY

ANY HAD FINISHED READING Martha's first doctoral thesis, a biblical exegesis with emphasis on the Exodus. It had raised a question for the hopeful entrepreneur: Would Moses be a good model for a tour business? The Egyptian-Jewish leader had spent forty years in the desert. Complaints, travel problems, bunions, food shortages, quarrels, factions, drinking water, dining spots, accommodations on the ground—he'd dealt with them all.

Yet in spite of his hardships, this historic leader still had the visionary power to daily remind travelers to focus their minds on God.

The violinist sat upright in his chair. On that cloudy morning, facing his window, watching the rain fall on the flowers in his garden, he summarized his existence by sending a volley of complaints heavenward: "My disappearance from the concert stage has gone far enough. I've disappeared even beyond disappearance. I've been totally forgotten—no one sees or recognizes me anymore. I'm returning to the ring. I want to get back in the fight, and once again hear voices of progress inside *and* outside my head.

"My armchair life was an acceptable existence—for an amoeba. But it is no longer acceptable for a *Zany!* Invisibility is over, done, complete, finished. Starting today I shall become a statement in CAPITAL LETTERS! A power thrust forward! I need praise and love. I'm ready to dive in again, to fend off the barbs of those who hate, despise, and taunt me. I'm older, more mature now. Who cares how others *feel* about me? . . . Well, I do, a bit. After a year of sitting with soul in hand, tossing it in the air, pocketing it, and generally getting to know the little fellow, I feel better. Period. Nevertheless, I still want the glow of audience validation. I need their eyes, ears, and recognition."

Zany stamped an exclamation point on the floor, emphasizing the power of his positive new attitude.

Saint James had been standing on the porch, surveying the garden and its many spring flowers. He entered the living room. Holding his rake in one hand and waving his green gardener's cap with the other, he shook his head in dismay. "I heard what you just said. Zoltan, that is *not* a business strategy or a marketing plan. 'Me, me, me. Ego, ego, ego.' It's the ranting of a maniac! You need guidance."

"I have celestial guidance."

"You need *earthly* guidance. You need business and marketing strategies. In other words, you need me!"

"You?"

"Me!"

"But you said 'Me, me, me. Ego, ego, ego' is not business plan."

"That's true, it isn't . . .when *you're* doing it." St. James raised his hat in the air. "But when *I* do it, it is! That's because my mind, skeleton, molecules, and every hunk of protoplasm in my body, have been ignited by the fire and knowledge of commerce!"

"How will that help *me?*"

"You'll see. First, you must work with me. Together we'll create the St. James and Zoltan Zany Entertainment Corporation."

". . .My name should come first."

"We'll figure out details later. Now is the time to make a decision: Take me on as a partner. You'll never get such a good offer again." St. James offered his hand to seal the bargain.

Zany hesitated. "This is all so sudden." He rose and began to pace the living room floor. "Let me think about it."

"Of course," St. James agreed. "Thinking is always good. But not too much, and not for too long. Remember, the best contemplation is done on your feet. Peripatetic is the way to go. It was good enough for Aristotle, and it's good enough for you. Pericles was also a peripatetic kind of guy who became an outstanding Athenian political leader by thinking on his feet. Such ambling locomotion is good for business, too! Especially business. Yes, Zoltan. A grand magyar *setalunk* plus an *Igen!* Walk, my lad, walk. Pace away! Burn up the rug with friendly foot fire. Consider my idea. Then grab it. But before you do, I'd suggest a solo walk around the block."

Dr. Zany agreed. He put on his brown bomber jacket, opened the front door, went down the brick stairs, and began a stroll through his neighborhood. The fresh spring air felt heavy with moisture. A faint scent of roses came from Rosy Carter's lawn next door. Passing the Victorian Paltwick home, Zany noticed a storm brewing overhead. Heavy black clouds roiled in the distance. The breeze turned into a chilling wind that sent a fierce warning of impending downpour. "No raincoat or umbrella," Zany said to himself. "I'm thoroughly unprepared for rain. But I don't care! I'm here to think about business!"

Suddenly, he heard a clap of thunder. A flash of lightning tore across the sky. The cloud burst above him. Torrential rain drenched his clothing. Standing in place, Zany concentrated on business and marketing as the downpour wiped his mind clean, preparing him for a fresh start.

The roaring wind blew the clouds across the sky. Soon a ray of sunlight peeked out. Focusing on the future, Zany looked upward, inward, forward, and back. Twenty-five years of concerts flashed before his eyes, followed by his dream of bringing beautiful violin playing to the world.

"I've done it! Thousands have heard my song. I've fulfilled my mission! I've won!" he exulted. "My task is complete! Thank God! Now I am *free!*" The wind howled, and the maple tree near him started to shake.

Zany glowed with happiness. Self-satisfaction combed his drenched body as he headed home.

For the next six months he ran victory laps around the local high school track field. One day, as he was panting with exhaustion after a six-mile run, another big question emerged: "What now?"

He was walking around the track again, dressed in running shorts and T-shirt, when a vision rose before him. Once more he saw a colorful crowd, tall, short, fat, thin, every race and religion, a pastel of people. All were drifting east, following their dancing leader to the mountain.

Zany sat down on the grass. He lay back and gazed at the sky. There he stayed for hours, smiling.

17

VIOLIN

S T. JAMES HAD JUST collected his four daily newspapers at Rockville's general store when he spied Dr. Zany at the door. "What are *you* doing here?" he asked. "I haven't seen you buy a newspaper for over a year! Have you thought about my business proposal? Shall we go into business together?"

"It's too early for that," Zany replied, reaching for the *Times*. "I'm still disoriented and lost." He scanned the headlines, paused, picked up the *Turkish Rodent*, a new English-Turkish magazine published by ex-patriots in Kusadasi, and licked his lips. "I'm here to stock up on sweets. Ah, the wonder of a halva bar bathed in chocolate!"

"Sounds metamorphic to me."

"Indeed, I have *been* transformed."

"Oh?"

"This morning I opened my violin case, tuned the instrument and, for the first time in over a year, I played the Bruch violin concerto. Such sweet sounds! Wild, powerful, and delicious. Then I worked on the Tchaikovsky and amazed myself by following it with Brahms, Mendelssohn, and Vivaldi."

"You're transforming yourself."

"Power, glory, and nobility are rolling with me! Playing these masters in magnificent fashion *is* my noble cause! From now on, I'm practicing violin in a totally new power-and-glory way. To achieve that, I need even more *practice!*

"The inner world must be conquered before the outward one can be approached," the Apostle concluded.

Search for
The Word

18

LEADERSHIP

D R. ZANY WAS SITTING in the Englewood, New Jersey, Starbucks, drinking coffee and reading *A Fiddler's Travel Guide to Mongolia* by Derrick Hoftalter. As he bit into his chocolate chip cookie, he spied a camel walking down Dean Street. One hump. Dromedary, no doubt. A man dressed in knee-length overcoat, sweeping cape, high boots, colorfully patterned stockings, leather pants, and a Tatra mountaineer's hat was leading the animal. He had a seeing-eye dog's leash in his right hand and a white cane secured by his thick black waist-belt. The man tied the camel to a parking meter, and, tapping his cane, started crossing the sidewalk towards Starbucks. After pushing open the glass door with his nose and foot, he turned right, aimed his dark glasses in Zany's direction, and sat down beside him. Turning away from the baffled violinist, he spoke in the opposite direction.

"*Dzien dobry. Milo poznac. Milo poznac.*"

"Are you speaking to me?" asked Zany.

"*Tak.*"

Zany's face scrunched into a question mark. "What language is that? I know it's not Hungarian."

The man straightened his glasses. *"Ja musz cwiczi. I happy to znac yu."* Pushing his dog to the side, he leaned his cane against the chair, and, in a deep, friendly voice, said, "Allow me to introduce myself. I am Poland man Zbigniew Pavel Tyreszius Kurlowkowicz. Friends call me Tyresziusz Pavel Koluboiuszczykowicz, but since you are not my friend yet, you can call me Freddie."

"Glad to meet you. . .Freddie." Zany extended his hand. "Welcome to Englewood."

"Dzienkuje bardzo, Dr. Zany."

"How do you know my name?"

"I recognize you anywhere, Doctor."

"But you're blind."

"The inner eye sees all." Raising his arm, the man summoned a waiter and ordered a coffee. Facing Zany, he continued, "Now, to the purpose of my visit. I want you make tour of my country."

"What do you mean?" Zany asked. "Me? I'm not a *tourist.* I'm an *artist.*"

"And a businessman, too."

A waiter brought the coffee. "Cream?" he asked.

"In my Poland country, we are black coffee people."

As a gesture of welcome and friendship, Zany took a sip of the man's coffee. He sighed a long, reflective sigh. "Well," he admitted, "what is a concert violinist but a businessman with fiddle in hand?"

"Exactly."

"Several years ago I toured Poland for three weeks as soloist with the New York Filled Harmonic Orchestra. I played Lalo's *Symphonie Espagnole* in Warsaw, Krakow, Lodz, Torun,

Gdansk, and even Olsztyn. But I've never led a tour group. What would such work entail?"

"You organize, you lead."

Zany nervously tapped out a Chopin polonaise with his foot. His mind had gone blank at such an idea. But after two bites of his chocolate chip cookie, a sugar rush caused his limping brain to emerge from its black hole and explore the possibility further. He gulped down his coffee as he thought: *Me? Lead?* I like the *word* 'leader.' But am I worthy of such a term? Do I have leadership skills? Such responsibility. Others look to you, want advice. Lost souls, empty and lonely, open themselves up, asking, begging, pleading to be led.

Freddie sensed the doctor wavering. He placed a hand of encouragement upon the violinist's shoulder. "You have more experience than you think."

"How do you know?"

"I see it in your eyes."

"But you can't. . .well, maybe it's true." Zany recalled past concerts. "For years I saw such eyes peering at me from the audience. Trusting faces, beseeching eyes filled with an innocent, other-worldly glow. They trusted my concerts. But a *leader?* Would they trust me to lead them? What models would I follow? Moses, Abraham Lincoln, Roosevelt, Sloan McGoogle, Winston Churchill. . . . I don't know."

Freddie tapped his cane, nodding while he listened.

Zany said, "Many artists create. Often they leave results of their vision in closets for years, sometimes forever. But a leader creates in the here-and-now. His art is performed with and through *others.*" Zany's felt his imagination warming up. The performer in him awoke. He rose and, raising his voice for other customers to hear, delcared, "The artist is a heroic leader! And vice versa!"

His new audience cheered. A bald man in checkered shirt shouted: "Go for it!"

A women with long black braided hair jumped up from her seat and bellowed encouragement: "Just shut up and do it!"

A law student, sitting in the corner behind his laptop computer screen, offered advice: "Only turds walk backwards."

Zany bowed to his audience. He sat down, leaned towards Freddie, and asked: "What sort of tour are we talking about?"

Three days later, Zany's pot of imagination was boiling, creating wild panoramas of Polish peasants dancing, castles looted by Eurasian hordes, horses galloping across the steppes, witches cackling in dark Lodzian forests, and birds humming gallant bagpipe cavalry tunes.

At the breakfast table, Martha was stirring oatmeal. "Then your program is all together?" she asked, spooning the porridge into his pre-heated bowl.

"I see the picture. Pieces are falling into place."

A wise Teutonic smile brightened her face. "Now the fun starts. Marketing begins!"

Zany's multi-dimensional brain moved easily and simultaneously in many directions. Nevertheless, these strange words brought it to a sudden halt. "Martha, are you crazy? Marketing *fun?*"

"Many happy people find it fun," she answered, pouring cream into his cereal bowl. "The creative part is developing a strategy, finding your fans, convincing others."

Zany shook his head in rebellion. To consider this once-dastardly deed as fun was revolutionary. He knew about art, technical prowess, creative direction. But to apply such things to mere commerce. . . ? In the old days, he would never have considered it.

But these were new days. Things were different. He thought about Starbucks, Freddie, tours, design, and the future of his inner art world. Michelangelo was painting on a new ceiling.

"What sort of tour will you run?" Martha asked.

Zany pushed his cereal bowl to the side. "I'm not sure yet. Freddie is waiting. The man is a seer even though he's blind. He says it's up to me to take the next step. The big picture will soon emerge. He wants my itinerary."

"Seering is good."

"Freddie said I can be of service to him."

"How?"

Zany stirred his cereal, brought a tablespoonful to his mouth, chewed and swallowed. Martha waited. "Through the peripatetic travel method. I got the idea from St. James, who got it from Aristotle. He told me about teaching at the ancient Lyceum in Athens, walking around, talking, and discussing." Martha reflected on her ancient Greek studies and Ph.D. thesis: *Second-Century Ptolemaic Influences on the Microbiotics of Nile Delta Plant Life.* Her brilliant analysis of pre-Cambrian mud embedded with newly discovered trilobite hair follicles had wowed the Butcher's Guild of Boston and graduate faculty at Harvard.

Dusting a back burner on the stove and slicing a carrot for the afternoon stew, she turned to Zany, "*Ja, mein Herr*, peripatetic is good," she said with satisfaction.

19

CONSULTATIONS

ZANY LOOKED UP: "WHERE have you *been*, Freddie?" "I appear when needed," came the reassuring answer of Zany's new consultant. "Your vacation has lasted long enough. Time to return to your roots. Otherwise, madness will overtake you."

Zany had been standing in the corner of his living room. Deep in thought, he glanced at his old armchair—dead, empty symbol of the past. Like a Roman relic, it reminded touring visitors of a once-glorious empire and transition into the Middle Ages. How would this violinist break the dusty spider web of old ideas? How would he move beyond the armchair life? The answer was so obvious he couldn't see it: Resurrection. Get back on the road of divine madness. Be true to the authentic Zany self.

"Transition has ended," said Freddie. "New life has begun."

"What will that life be?"

"We'll soon see," answered the blind, bearded seer. He leaned his shield on an adjacent chair, untied the Gordian knot of his shoelace, rose, fitted the helmet to his head, and raised his lance aloft. Pacing slowly across the living room rug, he declared: "All futures begin with clouds on the horizon."

"What's *that* supposed to mean?"

Freddie crossed his lance over his chest. "*I* shall be your nimbus, the new halo around your head."

"Oh?"

"You shall have a dual existence. As ye walk upon the earth, so ye shall walk in the clouds."

"*That* sounds weird."

"Ah, but Zoltan, my dear brainfry, your future grandchildren will not call you Grandweird for nothing. Best to combine Greek classics with French impressionists."

"What are you *talking* about?"

Creaking in his armor, Freddie reached for the coffee Martha had left on the chair beside him. "I'm not sure," he confessed, taking a sip, "but I know I'm on the right track."

"Freddie, how can you guide me when you know don't know where you're going?"

"Lost people make the best guides."

"You mean we should get lost together?"

"Precisely."

"Strange guidance."

"Of course. Hidden, strange, and unknown are the best kind. No one is exactly sure where they are going anyway. The lost realize this. I'll help you get there faster."

"What about *safety?*"

"You mean terrorism? There are two kinds, external and internal, threats from without and from within. Airport Security will handle external terrorism. I, as your resident psychologist, endorphin-fulfillment agent, Greek philosopher, and enthusiasm lifter, will provide you guidance for the *internal*."

"Okay. . . . What does *Greece* have to do with this?"

"We travel first through nightmares, the Hades of your past. Then we visit Elysian dreams of your future."

Zany's face brightened. "You mean we'll actually see that abode of the blessed? *Paradise itself?*"

Freddie rested a paternal hand upon Zany's trembling shoulder. "Calm yourself, my son. Naturally, these virtual abodes are part of our itinerary. Both are situated at the end of the world. But remember, Hades and the Elysian Fields— heaven and hell—are really the same place. Only our limited perspective views them as separate."

Zany's shoulders relaxed. Visibly impressed, he murmured, "Freddie, you *are* a wise man."

"Thank you. My partners agree."

"Partners?"

"I do not work alone. But more on that later. Now it's wake-up time. My friend, you need *caffeine* to jump-start your brain. Your double espresso at the Coffee Bean demonstrated that somewhere in that coffee high is where your future begins. Indeed a caffeine of adventure lies ahead." Freddie cleared his throat. "Speaking of ventures. . . ."

"I used to like adventures," Zany reflected. "But that seems so long ago, in the neolithic period of my pre-armchair life." He pondered in silent memories for awhile. Freddie sipped more coffee. Then the doctor's eyes widened. "What ventures are *you* talking about?"

The resonant voice of blind mentor boomed, "*Business* ventures."

"Business? Are you *nuts?*"

"First, we'll talk about ads and promotions."

"Ads? Never! Promotions? Forget it. I'm just not ready. Besides, I don't *do* business. I do art."

"Old language, Zoltan. Your protests are from a distant time. "You *did* art. In your next life, you'll do business—*and* art. Art skills will be applied to business, and business skills will be applied to art. Business will become your art, and art will become your business."

"You must be kidding."

Freddie raised his halberd. "As I *told* you somewhere in our short past, your next existence will include laughter, mirth, and joy."

"That sounds nice. Life in the here-and-now is good. But what about death?

"You can laugh at that, too."

"Disease, pain, suffering?"

"A bit more of a challenge. But with practice, and a dash of understanding and compassion, you can laugh at them as well."

Zany sucked on a tooth. Blood rushed to his brain; his heart pounded. Rising aortic joy, fueled by the intensity of future choices, possibilities, and directions was making him uncomfortable. To calm himself, he changing the subject. "Why do you wear medieval armor?"

"It protects me from my wife."

"Why don't you yell at her? That's what I did."

"Yes, that *is* what you did. And look where it got you. Now she lives in *Colorado*." Freddie stroked his helmet. "My wife, Janet, doesn't believe in emotional abuse. Only physical. Years ago she expropriated my long-handled gardening shovel. She took it from the garage and hung it on our kitchen wall. She began to call it her "house shovel." One day she picked it up and started swinging at me. Since I'm visually challenged, I couldn't see her swings coming. But when she finally found my thigh, I jumped. Next time she swung, I heard the swish of the wind and moved aside. She missed. I'm pretty fast once I hear the vibrations. That year I dodged every blow. But over time, with practice, she got faster. Her aim improved, too. I knew I needed protection. When I visited the Museum of Medieval History, I sensed a knight in full armor on display. Quietly I reached behind the glass case, felt the steel beneath my hand, and snatched his helmet. Wearing a steel protection helped a bit, but Janet's aim got even better. Soon I had to steal a full suit of armor. . . . But now we've worked it out. Things are better, and we're still together. A happy couple. These days, when Janet's upset and hits me over the head with the shovel, I don't feel a *thing*. Sure, the neighbors sometimes complain about the clanging. Still, it's a good workout for her. Builds upper body strength. Aerobic."

Zany looked appalled. "That's disgusting. Freddie. What about you? Stand up like a man. Hit her back."

"I never hit a woman."

"Just a couple of taps. . . ."

"Knights don't do that. I read the code in the museum. In the braille version, battering women is against the laws of chivalry. I refuse to disgrace myself and my fellow knights."

Zany invited Freddie for breakfast. Martha had whipped up a cabbage complete with onions, bacon, eggs, syrup, marmalade, and Ukrainian black bread.

Sipping his African-roast coffee, Zany asked his mentor, "Why did I wake up with a pain in my left foot this morning?"

Freddie leaned his pike against the wall, clanked to the sink, and washed off the soup ladle he'd used the night before to frighten away skunks lurking near the backyard garbage cans.

Returning to his seat, he answered, "You're starting out on a new path. New paths begin with the left foot." He stirred the orange juice in his mug. "Mystical podiatric studies show that placing the left foot in front of the right stimulates the unconscious. Most travelers are unaware of this effect. Growing pains in the left foot auger new horizons up ahead. My colleague and friend, the podiatric dentist Heinrich von Phutweir of Bavaria, refers to this as 'metatarsal madness.' The left foot secretly guides your new direction. That's why, as you grow and expand your consciousness, left foot pains that disappear are replaced by new ones."

Martha tapped a spoon on Freddie's forearm. "A fascinating explanation," she observed. "*You* are very *smart*."

"I agree," Zany concurred. "Infernally smart."

"I humbly thank you." Freddie knelt before Martha. He allowed her to pass a kitchen knife above his head, adding the Culinary Seal of Wisdom to his knightly collection. "I owe my wisdom and manners to my Italian education with Dante."

"Larry Dante, the Bolognese cook?" exclaimed Martha, her voice rising. "He was my mentor!"

"Not *that* one," Freddie sneered. "Dante Alighieri."

"Ah, yes. A second cook. But author of *The Eternal Inferno: Cuisine of Northern Italy*." He was a footnote in my Ph.D. thesis: *Medieval Florentine Cuisine*."

"Martha, I'm surprised at you," Zany snapped. "Everyone knows Dante Alighieri. A great athlete and violinist. He taught Pagannini how to play soccer."

"Idiots!" Freddie cried. "Dante's wrote the *Divine Comedy*. A masterpiece of allegory. Hell of a book, too. That man knew about heat. *Laurence* Dante Alighieri is one of his descendants. His Ph.D. thesis, *Dialogues Among 16th Century Frogs of Milan*, was published by the University of Padua Press three years ago. One month later, he caught PDT, a common post-doctoral thesis disease, and dropped his last name."

20

THE PLOTLESS LIFE

STILL CAUGHT BETWEEN THE old life and the new, haunted by the directional question, Zany once again asked, "Where am I going? Should I live for the future or dwell in the past?" He tugged at his white hair, brought his left hand into play, and began beating his head to a rouge-colored pulp in a orgy of self-flagellation.

Suddenly, he broke into a wide smile. Jumping up, he shouted to no one in particular, "What is my direction? *No direction at all!*" He pounded his chest with pride and happiness. "I know now! Yes! I'm a here-and-now guy. Today is where I am. Trade in becoming, exchange it for being—forward and backward are now the same!" To prove it, Zany muttered it to himself backwards "*Ma I erehw si yadot!*"

He ran down the stairs and into his garden. There he stood, tall, full, and free, surrounded by the blooming flowers and sky-breathing trees. Scents of roses and hydrangeas filled his spring nostrils. "My mind marvels at this spontaneous, serendipitous existence of going everywhere and nowhere at once." He watched the sun jump a bit higher in the sky. "What shall I call this new life?" He tore a leaf off the giant maple tree, waved it in the air, and triumphantly exclaimed: "I'll call it the *Plotless Life*."

Returning to the kitchen, he poured a glass of water, drained it halfway, and, to cool himself, dumped the remaining contents over his head. Bending to tie his shoe, he noticed ants crawling across the floor. "Martha!" he called. "*Feed* these creatures."

Martha scampered into the living room with a broom. She spotted the sandy formicator ant hill in the corner by the bureau. She scowled. "How did *they* get in here?"

"Ants arrive whenever my brain generates new ideas," replied Zany. "They are symbols of revitalized cerebral activity. Don't crush them, Martha. *Feed* them!"

"Quiet, Zoltan! You're a menace to cleanliness in this house. Ants carry diseases."

"But these are French ants."

"How do you know that?"

"Because of the way they formicate."

"Don't throw your French words at me." Martha charged at the ants with her broom. "No ants in this house!"

Zany retreated. "Calm down. They're only insects. Look how they busy themselves gathering grains of sand from the rug. These tiny creatures *enjoy* fulfilling their collective purpose, having fun doing their job."

Martha swept four ants into her dust pan. "Go back to your books," she hissed.

Zany raised his index finger pontifically. "Truth is, if you're having fun, you don't need books. Ants never read."

Martha studied him with skepticism and question marks in her eyes. "Zoltan, you need spice in your life, something more important than watching ants on the rug."

"You're right. I'm reaching that point. These ants appeared at this time for a reason. How graceful and purposeful they are. Look, they're actually dancing! Yes! Dancing on the job."

"Well. . . "

"Indeed, Martha, these could be the famous Romanian dancing ants of Calusvari! They've come to New Jersey all the way from Transylvania, the mother city of Cluj itself. My mother knew it as Kolozsvár, and my greatest of great dancing uncles, during his ancient Roman period, knew it as *Saltatio Claudioticum*, or the dancing medieval Latin city of Claudiopolis. Emperor Claudius, now *there* was an emperor who knew how to dance! . . . I'm sure these ants traveled first to Paris, then via a French freighter, to New York harbor, and finally to me! They point the way, *my* way! Study for *fun*."

Martha slowly shook her head. As she carried her pan full of ants to the kitchen sink, she said, "Zany, perhaps you had too little sleep. Your brain is fried this morning."

"Yes, and without oil. It's *about time!*" Like a bull released from his pen, he charged around the room. "I'm off. Dashing. Running. I'm on the right *road* now! Ants lead the way. Dance on, oh great Calusvari formilators!"

21

THE ROMANCE OF A COMPANY

R UN A COMPANY, THOUGHT Zany: Sink organizational energy deep into the earth, suck subterranean nutrients through irrational roots!

The romance of a company!

Name it *Babble International*. A universal company, Babbleonia as its emblem. Based on nonsense, adventure, and beauty. Can I do it? Will it work? What about staff? No wonder his back hurt.

What about a business plan? How about no plan at all? Why aim somewhere when you can go nowhere? And vice versa.

Zany sat at his desk, sweating and exhausted. He opened the Zany Curriculum Notebook, gripped the golden fountain pen sold to him by a Thracian merchant near Varna—the only pen, it was averred, flowing with Thracian ink used by Orpheus himself—and, across its empty pages, scribbled the substance of his business thoughts.

Between pages, to increase his blood circulation, he ambled over to the Rembrandt on his living room wall, plucked it from its hanger, turned it over and around in his hands, and fondly examined the artist's signature prominently displayed on the backing board: *Morris Rembrandt, Painting and Deli, 113 Delancey Street, New York.*

What about substance?

"Plotless! All directions are open. Our motto will be: Everything, anything, everywhere, and anywhere.

"It means travel, of course—Portugal, Serbia, China, Japan, Ecuador, Antarctica, the moon, the planets, the stars, anywhere! It means jazzy violin improvisations, wild words riding across the pages, twisted linguistics, strange etymological digs in the earth. It means—who knows what it means? But it *means!* I mean, *it means!*"

Sipping tea in the kitchen, Martha listened attentively. She sponged off the cutting board, pushed back her stool, and stepped into the living room to face the writing Zany.

"Only a strange, strong person can lead a directionless life." she said. "You *are* strange, Herr Doktor. But are you *strong* enough?"

"I'm strong." Zany rose from his seat and picked up a chair with his left hand. Holding it high above his head, he said, "You see, Martha, my fingers are powerful from years of practice. Nothing strengthens arms and shoulders more than playing Bach, Mozart, Mendelssohn, Saint-Saens, Lalo, and Bruch for hours on end. Nevertheless, you raise an interesting point. Am I strong *enough?* If I am not, how do I *get* stronger? How can I lead the directionless life of my company with dignity, power, and conviction?"

"Practice."

"Precisely! Practice perfected my violin skills. Practice will lead to perfecting the Plotless Life. Exercises open, expand, strengthen, and loosen the joints of my mind. But what exer-cises? Where can I find them?"

He put down his chair and stood before the dinner table in silence. Martha sat down in his old armchair, leaned back, and took another sip of tea. A ring of thought-provoking stillness engulfed the living room.

Finally, she said, "Herr Doktor, you'll need a staff."

22

GENGHIS KOHAN

THREE WEEKS LATER, ZANY was standing opposite Genghis Kohan, former orthodox rabbi of Beth Mizrach Hagadol and head of the synagogue and congregation in the Mongolian capital of Ulan Bator. Although short by Western standards—measuring four feet seven inches—Kohan's deep bass voice, coupled with powerful abdominal muscles, enabled him to hurl forceful invectives. The man's vast self-confidence and ability to pronounce umlauts correctly impressed Zany, who ushered the Mongolian leader towards the interview seat. "Please, sit down," Zany said.

"I do not sit during daytime hours," Kohan emphasized.

"May I offer you tea?"

Kohan shook his head. "No daytime liquids either. But if you have a slice of horse meat, I'll take it."

"Martha, my house keeper, never serves that," replied Zany. "How about a hamburger?"

"Never mind," snapped the Mongolian. "I can't wait all day. Let's get to work." His sharp black eyes narrowed analytically, thick powerful neck muscles rotating his small head. Visually, he inspected Zany's office. "Why did you invite me?" he asked.

Zany sat in his swivel chair, put his feet on the newly installed mahogany desk, and, trying to appear professional, in control, confident, yet casual, said, "I'm starting my first company. I want to learn how to become an entrepreneur. When I looked up the word 'entrepreneur' in the telephone book, your name came up first."

"Strange book."

"All my telephone books start with the fifth letter. Prune the alphabet to fit you, that's what my mother taught me." Zany reached for a pencil and pad of interview paper. "Please, Mr. Kohan, tell me about yourself."

Ghengis leaned against the wall and raised his arms in an archer's stance. "My birth certificate says *Larry Cohen*. But since childhood, I've admired the war tactics of the Central Asian hordes, especially Attila the Hun, Tamerlane, and the great Ghengis Khan himself. That's why I Mongolianized my name. 'Genghis' reminds me of capitalism, war, and entrepreneurial practices."

"I didn't know that about Mongolians." Zany scribbled all this on his notepad. "Go on."

Ghengis moved away from the wall, rocked on the balls of his feet in order to drive powerful thoughts all the way up to his cerebellum, a challenging task even under ideal conditions, and explained. "Rocking in place is part of the Mongolian speaking style. Genghis Khan himself was small in stature. Same as me. Yet he led his people to victory across eleven time zones. As with him, atomic-powered electrons create energy explosions within me. That's why clients call me the 'Mongolian Molecule.'"

"Before you go on with your personal history," Zany interrupted, "I'd like to bring St. James into this interview. He's good in business."

"Later, later," Genghis objected. "The Apostle's input will help coordinate our orthodox Western business view."

"How do you know his title?"

"Businessmen in Western Mongolia are familiar with the James exploits. But my own entrepreneurial talents incline towards Central Asia. I follow the Wild-Horsemen-of-the-Steppes approach. It is similar to the one your Hungarian ancestors took before they crossed the Carpathian Mountains. As you may know, Attila the Hun, before he conquered Europe, had a side business selling flowers from the Orkhon River. *Temujin Tulips.* And he performed this entrepreneurial feat in spite of his father Yesugei's insistence that no tulips grew in the Khangai Mountains, or anywhere in Mongolia."

"I didn't know that."

"There are many things you don't know." Kohan pulled a cigarette from his pocket. "But this didn't stop little Genghis." He struck a match on his foot, lit his cigarette, clenched his fists, and growled. "It won't stop me, either!"

The powerful thrust of Kohan's unexpectedly aggressive response stabbed Zany's brain and heart, releasing a surge of high alert wakefulness. A cloudy mixture of rage, worry, ambivalence, wonder, and despair gripped his soul.

Why now? Going into business was so new. Was there no escape from the anxiety it created, the discomfort and fear of entering its unknown maw? Yet the attack persisted—and in the middle of a *business interview!* How could he make an impression on Kohan when ghostly fingers of such dark trepidation lurked within?

Could this be the famous entrepreneurial rage? Dr. Photo-synthiatikos had mentioned it in his study of the Minotaur, *Cretan Myths and Mysteries*. As a violin soloist traveling across the world, Zany had paid scant attention to such energy concepts. After all, he had been an *artist*, not a businessman, and certainly not an entrepreneur. Decisions affecting the material world had been left to his agent and concert manager. But now, as he entered a new world of business, he felt vaguely lost and alone. How did this entrepreneurial thing *work*, anyway?

Suppressing a glare, he eyed Kohan, rose from his desk, and felt a shooting pain in his meniscus. He limped to the right, hobbled, leaned on his desk, and sat down as weird start-up pains attacked his left knee. What would *Mother* think, to say nothing of the Mongolian Molecule?

"Pardon my hobble," he said to Kohan.

"Don't mention it. Most new businesses begin with a hobble."

Kohan sat on Zany's desk, held the doctor's hand, and looked him straight in the eye. "Relax. Nothing to worry about. Leading with a limp is the way to go. Even the famous Genghis Khan hobbled before his first invasion of Europe. All leaders hobble at first." The Molecule removed a handkerchief from his pocket, wiped Zany's forehead, and related an apt episode from Mongolian history.

23

BUSINESS MEETING

"P OPPLECOCKELMIRE SIGRETS NO MORE!" Kohan sounded definitive.

"What's that supposed to mean?" St. James asked.

Zany had taken off his socks. Fidgeting with his feet, he massaged his big toe, hoping to find an inspiring business idea.

The first business meeting of Zany's venture had begun on May Day. Proletarian flowers were already blooming. The partners gathered in his living room. St. James flung himself across an armless chair, his tall, thin frame wrapped in a blanket; a woolen Faeroe Island knit hat sat on his head, keeping his brain cells warm, fluid, and ready to leap into action at a moment's notice.

Kohan had fallen asleep on the couch. He used this proto-Mongolian warrior slumber tactic to gather and focus mental forces in preparation for the battle ahead.

Zany folded his legs in half-lotus position before the fireplace. "Martha," he called. "Bring the boys a glass of water from our sump pump."

"That is impolite, Herr Doktor. It is unwise to offer such dubious waters. Instead I'll bring fresh-squeezed juice from our Florida oranges."

"Good idea," answered Zany. "Orange sugar heightens energy. Such fluids, filled with rich sub-soil nutrients, strengthen mind and invigorate the soul. Exploring a new material reality is no easy task."

Zany looked at his business team. A belch of pre-Nestorian cosmic creativity, coupled with delicious sadness, pumped through his chest. His mind began to separate from his body— a familiar, comforting sign. Years of concert performances had made him well acquainted with the down before the dawn. He sensed a rebirth coming fast.

He rose. Jolts of lambent energy channeled through his material self. Eyebrows danced. Pounding his violin fist on the coffee table, the commander of this new regiment exclaimed, "Boys, I'm ready! Let's get to it. What business shall we choose?"

St. James took a sip of water. "You're the boss. It's your choice."

"*My* choice?" Zany retreated, a puzzled look on his face. "But you are my *advisors!*"

Kohan spoke up. "My master said, 'Choose your path! Hordes shall follow.' It's the Mongolian Way."

Zany considered his new position. He was in charge. He leaned back in his swivel chair and gazed at the ceiling, hoping stray ideas might fall from heaven. "Let's apply artistic principles to the business world," he finally said. "I want a concert of beauty in the entrepreneurial universe. Our goal is to synthesize opposites, unite heaven and earth!"

"A lofty goal," said St. James.

Zany swooned. "What would mother say?" he muttered in sotto-voce reflection. "And Papa, too. How pleased they must be to hear their reborn, entrepreneurial son expostulate; how happy it must make them in their posthumous dwelling near Uranus. I'll phone them tomorrow. I'm happy about it, too. What a magnificent purpose ours will be!"

"Drop the 'will be,'" St. James protested. "*Is* is the word that nails the present. We start today!"

"*Will be* is even *better!*" declared Kohan. The Mongolian Molecule raised his fist like a flag. "The present sucks. The future is ours! Let it drive us onward, upward, and sideward!"

Zany smiled, nodding his approval.

St. James held the floor. "Obviously, a *general* vision of business is needed. However, we must be more specific. Zoltan, what *kind* of a business do you want?"

Kohan concurred. "Service or production oriented?"

Zany rubbed his eyes.

"You like planting," St. James offered. "How about vegetables?"

"*You* are the one who likes planting," Zany reminded him.

"Transportation is important," Ghengis said. "How about rubber tires? That's what Kublai, even Tamerlane, would choose today if they were here."

Zany looked doubtful. "Kohan, what do rubber tires have to do with music?"

"The name is *Genghis!* Especially during business meetings."

"All right, all right. Still, rubber tires, Genghis. . .it just doesn't sound right."

"See how quickly you rejected tires?" St. James pointed out. "They lack sonar significance. Although you spent a year in your armchair trying to escape your performing career, *music* is still in your soul."

Martha entered, carrying a pitcher of orange juice. Zany stroked his chin while she filled the glasses. Massaging his molars, the violinist turned to his house manager. "This all sounds so sensible, Martha. What do you think?"

Martha mumbled something about Byzantine bath water and seventh-century Greek porridge before leaving the room.

Genghis straightened in his chair. "I agree with St. James. Music should be part of your new business. There wasn't much melody and song during the Mongol conquest. Lots of screaming."

"Didn't Kublai Khan like Chinese music?" St. James asked.

Zany dug his fingers into his thigh. "Enough about Mongolia! Who cares about the Mongols, anyway?"

Genghis grabbed Zany, threw him to the floor, and fixed his black boot on the doctor's neck. "How *dare* you!" he cried. "Never, *never* insult my tribe!"

"Okay, okay." Zany pushed off the Mongolian.

"This is ridiculous," said St. James. "Let's get back to business."

Genghis nodded. "Sorry about that," he said. "I'm sensitive to historical injustice."

Zany rubbed his neck. "Aren't we all? Forgiven and forgotten. Let's move on. What business?"

24

NEXT BUSINESS CHAPTER

LOST AND DIDDERHOTS! THAT'S the way Zany felt as the sun of a new day shone into his bedroom. Slipping out of his lambswool pajamas, freshly imported from the Himalayas by an ex-sherpa friend, concert violinist Tenzin Paypelapete, the doctor covered his naked body with a Walmart bathrobe and shuffled across the rug into the bathroom. Although groggy, his mind full of dreams, he managed to urinate with great skill, shuffle to the sink, wash his face with a towel purchased in Kusadasi from a Turkish marketer, Selim the Magnificent, clean his teeth, polish each molar, brush his mane of white hair, ease a cramp in his right leg, burp, and pat his abdomen. When finished, he headed to the kitchen for coffee and fresh start. The first cup of Martha's morning Columbian brew stimulated somnambulant blood cells, turning them into high-speed work demons whose fiery locomotion from metatarsal to metacarpal to mandibular snapped his brain to attention. Mind prepared, he readied himself for the second business meeting.

Standing at the edge of change, once again panic seized him. Jaws clamped down on the corpse of his former self. How do you start over? Where to begin? Would he like Martha's cuisine? Would a new Zany remain zany? What about his charm, vitality, energy? If he changed his career, would these qualities remain with him? And the thin line between sanity and insanity? As an entrepreneur, would he dwell in the core of divine madness that had energized his artistic life?

"I'm sick of my mind!" he sighed. "I'm especially sick of my fears! They've haunted me enough. In fact, I'm so sick of my trembles, I'm dumping them!"

He shook his shoulders with all his strength. Forty-seven fears fell out.

Dr. Zany straightened up. Emboldened by new pride, he opened his closet, and pulled out the polished black business shoes purchased for him by St. James during his 2006 North Africa concert tour. An entrepreneurial moment had occurred on their visit to the souk in the southern Tunisian city of Gabes. Zany had exhibited nascent haggling skills while purchasing the primitive Tunisian bagpipe, a *medwin*. St. James had been amazed when the violinist picked up the sagging instrument, turned it over, examined its rank underside, blown through its chanter, and asked the shopkeeper, "How much?"

The gaunt salesman had smiled underneath his moustache and said, "Forty dinars."

Zany had winced, looked at the *medwin* again, and run away.

The salesman had immediately run after him, shouting, "Thirty, thirty."

Zany'd kept running, the salesman on his heels.

"Twenty-five, twenty-five!" Street had faded into street. "Twenty! *Twenty!*"

After running through what seemed half of Gabes, Zany had

stopped, the salesman had panted to a halt, and they'd agreed on a price of two dinars.

As Zany slipped into his business shoes, he remembered the thrill of that chase. "Running for a bargain," Martha called it. He tied his shoes, stood up, threw back his shoulders, and strode into the living room office.

An hour later, St. James was sitting opposite him. "The way I see it, Zoltan," he said, "even though you run well, your skills, talents, and interests lie in music. Your business should involve music."

"I agree," said Genghis. "Follow your skills. It is the path of the Mongolian horseman."

St. James pointed to Zany's feet. "You're wearing business shoes! Obviously you remember Tunisia and your bargaining abilities."

"Mongolians like to bargain, too," Genghis added.

Zany considered these directions. When the flow of thoughts pooled peacefully in his mind, he leaned forward. "Okay. We'll include music. But this time it will be something different."

"During your years of concert career travels," said St. James. "I never heard you complain about sea sickness, air plane flights, or even horse-driven cart rides through the Balkan mountains. I thought you handled the Shipka Pass landslide commendably. You're a good traveler."

Genghis jumped in. "Mongolians love travel. You could combine *travel and music.*"

Zany's eyes brightened. "Now there's a good idea."

He remembered how, during his last concert in Antwerp, three lunatics on a field trip from the local mental health clinic had jumped up and down in the aisles, screaming with happiness. After the concert, the director of the clinic had even come backstage and offered him a job! What a night! When he completed the final movement of the Wienawski, the audience, had cheered wildly, then risen and stood, shouting and applauding, for three days—the longest standing ovation on record!

Or so it seemed. Zany remembered pain in his feet from standing so long, his lower back ache from bowing, and the dryness in his lips from repeating, "Thank you," thousands of times. He had re-experienced the ache in his groin from performing his backward bow countless times.

He had developed this bow after a concert in Madagascar, when the audience, mad with passion, would not stop cheering. The audience would not leave, even after he bowed over forty times and returned to the stage for his fourteenth encore, the Paganini *Moto Perpetuo*. Exhausted, he'd turned his back to the audience and spontaneously bowed backwards. The audience had hardly noticed it. They'd just kept cheering.

Since that night, Zany had incorporated the backward bow after concert encores. Considering its success, he'd soon begun to *give* his concerts backwards. Then the audience *had* noticed, and many had begun to walk out. By that moment in his career, after several years of suffering from concert and touring fatigue, Zany had been desperate to end the grueling routine. When he saw audiences leaving, he'd continued backward programs. After a year, his audience had diminished to ten, then five, souls. Finally, when the numbers hit zero, his management, Gilded Concert Associates, had decided to drop him.

This had given Zany plenty of free time to think about his past, present, and future. He'd sat in his armchair for a year. But the long silence had ended. He was back in a game. The only question now was: *What game?*

St. James reflected further. "I like it. Genghis is right. Music and travel: Such a business combination would work."

Martha served the staff cups of Columbian coffee flavored with jumping java pepper meat powder, Attila's favorite morning additive.

Finally, Zany clapped his hands. "I have it!" He jumped to his feet in happy illumination. "A music travel company!"

St. James grinned. "The *both* solution. Good!"

Genghis's voice was tinged with excitement: "I envision hordes of traveling musicians, even musical pillagers, wilding across the globe, tearing up cities, wrecking towns, burning down farms, ripping up gardens, leveling forests, leaving an incomparable wake of destruction in their path. My Mongolian forebears would be proud."

"I hadn't quite envisioned *that*," said Zany. "But there *would* be traveling involved."

25

ATTILA'S SEARCH BEGINS

AFTER GRADUATION, ATTILA FOUND a position as Director of the Linguistics Department at the University of Bone-upon-Maine. There, as head of the word-root research committee, he continued speculation on the origin of language. The science, art, history, archaeology, and etymology of word roots had fascinated him ever since age four, when an inability to pronounce the letter "t" had caused words like *truth*, *turnip*, or *tear* turned into *root*, *roornip* and *rear*.

Presently, he was sitting on the morning flight to Spain. Staring out the window from his tourist-class seat, reflecting on his past, he realized his primal vision of peace, security, and transcendence had begun, not with his discovery of ancient civilizations, but earlier, in his room at home, his personal Garden of Eden.

Indeed, that was why ancient civilizations made sense, why the mystery of the Hittites, Hurrians, Assyrians, Babylonians, and Sumerians, the Hebrews and Canaanites and Egyptians, all fell into place.

Attila gazed again at the clouds drifting by. He knew he'd

never find word roots meditating on a plane. Yet secretly, he hoped to find proof of an ancient theory claiming the origin of language lay, not on Earth, but in heaven. This idea had been recently reformulated as the Celesto-Centric Theory of Centrifigal Root Force by the man he was flying to meet, the eminent Israeli etymologist, Haifa-born, Tel Aviv beach-raised Isaac "Cookie" Mashugi. The professor's linguistic laboratory, Milon Ha Rishon, had been constructed in 1984—from verbs, nouns, and an assortment of curses—both in his basement and at Kibbutz ha Pe, located in the Judean desert just west of Masada. There, with an occasional southward glance towards Sodom and Gomorra, Mashugi had delved into word origins, trying to find the original proto-Ur word, the *milon ha rishon*, first grunted by primitive man hundreds of thousands of years ago.

The professor believed that thousands of such Ur-words could be found in Noah's ark, which, he believed, was located on Mt. Ararat. By digging deeply into its ancient contents, he hoped to find, not only a few syllables, but the very first sound uttered of man himself! Such a discovery would overshadow even the Dead Sea Scrolls. Demand for lectures would rise, and he could finally head the World Language Association's annual meetings.

The pilot announced the plane was out of fuel and they'd have to make a crash-landing in a Madrid suburb. Attila preferred an earlier disembarkation. He grabbed a parachute, pushed a frantic flight attendant out of the way, and headed for the door.

Twenty-three minutes later he landed in a tree at the edge of a Madrid gypsy camp. Brushing off his clothes to the sound of a flamencan guitar playing *Bulerias*, he realized that, indeed, language had had its origin in God's mouth and had been passed from Him down to Earth for man's use. A few of the dancers and gypsy musicians wandered over to greet him. He thanked them for their music, made his way to the Prado Museum, stepped into a phone booth next to a Velazquez painting, and phoned Mashugi.

"I'm on my way. Finally!" he exclaimed. "My approach is celestial, yours terrestrial. We'll make a good team."

"Crazy," Mashugi shouted gleefully into the phone.

Two months later, flying a DC-9 from Istanbul to Van in eastern Turkey, the research team headed to Mt. Ararat. High on the mountain top, in the ancient mouth of Noah, they hoped to find the "Aah" sound of wonder that, Mashugi believed, was the origin of all languages.

"We need a hotel," said Mashugi upon arrival at the Van airport. "Or should we sleep in his ark tonight?"

"Material needs come second," said Attila. "We'll be there soon. Then we'll start our project and find *him*."

"Have you ever considered the difference between writing and vomiting?" asked Mashugi. "Three weeks ago I met the great cartologist Norman Proctol. He warned me of pendulous difficulties ahead, how great breasts of fire have burned former travelers on the route of Great Bonding. These whale-whoppers smash their ripe, rotund appendages against man's flaccid brain, creating heat centers, sparks, and fires. They turn brave, adventurous ideas to ashes. Thus our minds must struggle to remain straight and firm, like the prehistoric consciousness of Firmicus Erectus, whose hectic Dionysian clatter used the Italo-Dinosaurian dialect of Lillylinguinni."

Attila nodded. "I'm glad you said that, Isaac." He placed his hand on Mashugi's shoulder. "Now calm down."

Mashugi removed his glasses. "Our search must include re-search, post-search, and posterior search. We cannot let fallow bottoms lie. *The Book of Lambadromedaries,* by Lawrence McWeek, lists many of our challenges on its missing page four-teen. Our trek must first overcome the Great Asia Minor Hiss-ing Sound, located somewhere outside of Konya. This serpentine gasp of bilabial negation has slithered about for cen-turies, nearly squeezing Asia Minor out of geographical exis-tence. It now threatens to destroy modern Turkey and the rest of the world.

"Any lilliputian phlogiston theory can be applied to linguis-tics, especially italo-linguistics, since most linguists languish on linguini, sprinkled with psychosis and sauced with metamorphic bottled schizophrenia whose metempsychosis turns all base met-als into gold. These theories, often hidden in wetlands or subsoil end brains, can be harmless or lethal. . .depending on the spelling."

"Remarkable," sighed Attila. "I never knew!"

26

MICRO-RUNNING AND TAMERLANE

BACK AT HIS RIVERDALE home, Zany's leg system collapsed as another earthquake of doubt revisited him. Was he on the right trail? By giving up his self-definition as an artist, violinist, and performer, would he plunge into an abyss of emotional meaninglessness?

Claustrophobia set in—suffocation, a heavy heart, shortness of breath. He knew that feeling! *Repression!*

He was squashing possibilities of a *business high,* pushing down joy itself. After all, couldn't off-the-wall, crazy, wild, and exciting moments be found in *marketing madness?*

It felt right. Yes. Reaffirmed at last! Just as his artistic self had found fulfillment in performing concerts, so his entrepreneurial marketing self could find the joy in business.

What did art and business have in common? *Madness!*

The doctor smiled. A joyful scream broke from his lips. Positive vibrations bounced around the living room as he shouted "Wahooo!" A transformed Zany jumped from his chair, sprang into the air, and clicked his heels.

Genghis and St. James looked on in happy amazement.

"Lads, I can't stand sitting anymore! Let's *get out of here!*"

"Zoltan, what progress you have made," St. James said proudly. "Except for the fire and a few walks, you haven't left your house for a *year*. Moving from your armchair to the living room used to be a major step. Now *this? Leave the house?* What a colossal jump!"

"Had this been a problem?" Kohan asked.

Ignoring the question, Zany turned to the door. "Yes, guys, I'm tired of sitting. I'm even tired of standing. Let's *move!*"

He grabbed the doorknob, yanked the door open, banging his head on the frame, and charged through. "Follow me!"

"Should we bang our heads, too?" asked Kohan.

"Of course," Zany answered, dashing down the steps and into the street. With his staff race-walking behind him, trying to catch up, Zany shouted back, "It's a pre-concert technique I once used. It stimulates the pituitary gland, increases energy, and conquers fear."

"I never heard of such a thing," St. James panted.

Moving his hands in rapid circular motion to stimulate blood and enthusiasm, Zany turned to the Apostle. "Try it. You'll see. One bang gives you minimal benefits, seven bring relief, and fourteen make you feel *great.*"

Kohan tapped his head lightly on a maple tree; St. James, remembering a similar technique from his gardening days, followed with three hearty blows.

"It's so beautiful outside," Zany cried. "What wonderful fresh air, sky, and sun! What could be better?"

"I'm a clouds man," Kohan wheezed.

The three walked around the block and returned to Zany's office. Trees and flowers still beckoned. They waited on the sidewalk for further instructions. "What shall we do now?" St. James asked.

"Run," replied Zany.

"Run?" Kohan froze. "I never run."

"Zoltan, you're returning to your old ways," said St. James, remembering. "I like it. Where shall we run?"

"I *never run*," Kohan repeated. "It is not the Mongolian way. Give me a horse. I can ride forever. Running is beneath me."

"Try it, Genghis," Zany encouraged. "Think about history. Kublai Khan would be proud of you. Besides, I don't run in the traditional sense."

Kohan looked skeptical. "What does that mean?"

"I'll tell you," Zany replied, leaning on his story-telling leg. "As a precocious, wild, and zoo-released four-year-old, I loved lawn-dashing."

"Lawn-dashing?" remarked St. James, leaning against a lamppost. "That's a new one. I never heard that word. What could it be, my frail power?"

Zany stooped to tie his shoe. "It expresses the sad mosaic of my childhood years. Mama and Papa Zany, avatars of my youth, repressed my animal instincts and psychological needs. To escape, I often stole from the second floor of our suburban home and hustled across the street to run with wild abandon in the park. I took off my shoes and dashed like crazy! The grass felt so *good* as it brushed past my naked feet! My soul-bottom bloomed with praise!

"There I discovered archaeological wounds deep in my unconscious subsoil. Frequently I wrapped myself in a cloud of ineffable longing."

"As a child of *four?*" Kohan asked.

"Indeed. Some say life begins at birth. But Mama Zany claimed it began at four. She stood in the doorway, shouting her philosophy at neighbors across the street."

"Is this why you are hobbling?" Kohan tightened his belt. "Your pace reminds me of Genghis Khan, and his early life in the forest steppes."

"Yes. But it is not hobbling. Rather, it is a running style of my own invention called *micro-running*. I discovered it one summer day at Cape Cod. What a vacation *that* was! I had been suffering from a foot injury, gastrotenditis of the metapscyhotarsal, a severe swelling of the tonsilo-fibular band."

"I never heard of that condition," said St. James.

"Stick to money, my apostle. Obviously, you're not a runner. Anyway, I hadn't run for two weeks. One day, in my frustrated condition, I saw a runner in shorts and T-shirt dash past my window. How sad it made me feel. Why couldn't *I* do that? My resolve hardened. I decided to run even if I could only move at a snail's pace! Anything was better than staying in the house, moping. So I put on my sneakers, shorts, and T-shirt, walked out the door, stepped into the street, and started to run . . .very, very *slowly*. Slow, slow, slow. I ran almost in place. I waved to a woman in the house across the street. She waved and returned to her house cleaning. I kept putting one slow foot in front of another, going almost nowhere. Twenty minutes later, I had hardly moved. The woman appeared in the window again and waved. I waved back, feeling somewhat embarrassed. Yet something strange had happened. I'd begun to break into a soft sweat. Even better, ever so slowly, muscles in my feet had begun to warm up. As they did, my pain subsided. Progress: I started moving minutely forward. An hour later, I had gone one block. Yet by then, by some miracle, the pain had totally disappeared!

'Amazing,' I said. 'I've made a discovery.' A motto rose in my brain: 'The last shall be first.' I pictured medieval Mongolian hordes galloping across the Central Asian plains." Zany pumped his clenched digits towards the blue sky. "At heart I am a *warrior*," he cried. "Ventricle and aorta trill, tittle, and hobble towards power. *Toe glory* is my battle cry!"

"Toes are quite masculine," said Kohan, commenting from his knowledge of Mongolian history. "Tamerlane himself was a toe man. He suffered from metatarsal mania. The origin of his name is Persian. *Timur-i-lang* means 'Temur the Lame'"

"I didn't know that," said St. James as they ran past Cable Street. "You're quite a scholar."

Kohan tightened his belt another notch. Micro-running was beginning to take effect. Beads of sweat had appeared on his forehead. "I have studied my mentors' lives for many years. Tamerlane was my childhood hero. I remember 1941, when his body was exhumed by the Russian scientist Gerasimov. After examining the skeleton, this researcher not only confirmed my leader's lameness but found his height to be five feet eight inches."

"You actually read *books* on this?" asked St. James.

"Of course. I studied Gerasimov's *The Face Finder*. In it this fastidious scholar explains how he reconstructed the exact likenesses of Timur by examining his skull. Another Ulan Bator professor, Sharaf ad-Din, claims that Timur, while stealing sheep in his twenties, received arrow wounds. This left him with a lame right leg and stiff right arm for the rest of his life. Tamerlane made light of these disabilities." Kohan sighed in pagan pleasure worship. "What a guy!"

They ran past Stone Street.

"He never gave up," Kohan continued. "By 1369, Tamerlane was proclaimed sovereign at Balkh."

"Balkh?" Zany jumped in. "*That* dump? I gave a concert there five years ago. After my concert, not one person applauded. I have never been greeted by such total silence."

"Balkh people are sensitive to music," Kohan explained. "They love sonatas executed correctly. Perhaps you played too many wrong notes."

"Never!"

Retreating into silence, the runners passed Bard Street. When Mortimer's Deli appeared on the corner, Zany burped with rage. Somehow the sight of hot dogs hanging in the window released of old memories. "On my 1994 concert tour of Afghanistan," he recalled, "I played the Bruch violin concerto I with a local orchestra in Balkh, or 'Wazirabad,' as my local manager called it. Afterwards, Bedwin Hasan met me backstage." He motioned to St. James with his thumb. "At six foot nine, he stood a good three or four inches taller than you. 'Americans call me Big Al,' he said. "'Al'" means "'the'" in Arabic, so my Turkic-speaking kinsmen, who also know Arabic, call me "'Big The.'" He reached into his pocket, pulled out a faded business card, and handed it to me. *Astrophysicist and Consultant to the Stars.* 'What stars have you consulted with?' I asked. 'Many,' he answered. 'John Wayne, Carole Lombard, or Barbara Streisand?' I asked. 'How about Vince Lombardi, Gertrude Highburn, Robert Redford, Priscilla Hogbenflufer, Fladberg Koppelstein, or Rudolf Giuliani? Anyone *I* know?'"

"'I do not consult with *earthly* mortals,' Al sneered. 'Although sometimes I do individualized work with red supergiants such as Betelgeuse, the Arabic House of Twins, or Alpha Andromedae. No, I work primarily with groups; I consult with constellations—Orion, The Big Dipper, or The Great Utensil, or a little known one 40 billion light years away. Many of the stars I meet feel lost in the universe. So do planets that fall out of orbit periodically and lose their way. They need guidance and direction.'"

"You still missed some notes," Genghis grumbled.

"I never—"

"Stop!" commanded St. James. "Running and arguing don't mix. Focus on your feet."

They passed State Street, glancing at the blue sky above while suburban homes in hues of yellow, gray, and white flowed by.

"What about Tamerlane's mind?" St. James asked as they ran under the Bander Avenue sign. "Did he have any brains?"

"Ha, you and your Santiago de Compostela, Lugo, and post-Galician arrogance!" sneered Kohan, tripping over a pot hole. Recovering his stride, he raised his scholarly index finger. "Timur had *extraordinary* intelligence, with an intuitive approach. Although he couldn't read or write, he nevertheless spoke Persian and Turkic. At mealtimes, he heard stories about history. This leader appreciated architecture and gardens. In fact, Timur loved art so much he often stole it! That's why the Byzantine palace gates of the old Ottoman capital Brusa were removed and carried off to Samarkand."

"Very nice, for a pagan," said St. James.

They spied Biteoff's Delicatessen Store on Hazel Avenue in the distance. A hydrant painted white by the fire department to symbolize purity stood to their right. Kohan touched it for good luck before answering, "By mentioning 'pagan,' you raise in interesting point. "For hundreds of years, Timur's religious beliefs have been controversial. After much study and research on my own part, I'd say they were Turco-Mongolian shamanistic with an added touch of Sufi. Even more important for us in the modern world, Tamerlane appreciated diversity. His army consisted of Muslims, Christians, Turks, Tajiks, Arabs, Georgians, and Indians. They all worked together pillaging, raping, destroying cities and whole civilizations. During every massacre, he remained a devout multiculturalist!"

"I thought you were talking about Timur," said St. James. "Who is Tamerlane?"

"Timur, Tamerlane, same thing," answer Kohan. "Here in the West, he is commonly known as Tamerlane."

"I'm a mono man myself," Zany put in. "But, Genghis, my friend, what does Mongol history have to do with *business*, especially the one we're trying to build?"

The Church Street sign loomed ahead as their pace accelerated. "Tamerlane also had a great interest in commerce and trade," Kohan replied. "He wanted to monopolize commerce between Europe and China by controlling travel routes on the Silk Road. As for business technique, he used war. Unfortunately, his health deteriorated. February 18, 1405, he died."

The men ran on in silence for another half hour. Upon reached Zany's home, St. James said, "Let's take a business break."

"Agreed," the others answered simultaneously,

Kohan headed to the deli for a bite to eat; St. James lay under a tree in the garden. Zany entered the living room, opened his violin case, tenderly lifted his fiddle, and tucked it under his chin. He swayed gently as he began playing a Bach *partita*.

27

DREAM OF ATTILA

"OLD EXPLANATIONS ARE DEAD," said Zany. He put the violin back in its case. "I need new names for notes. Chord progressions, too." He scratched his nose; a noun fell out.

Martha entered the living room. In one hand, she was carrying Zany's cup of afternoon tea. In the other, to honor the birth of the new business, she had an additional side plate of cookies and a doughnut. "Here's what to do," she counseled. "Stick to the bass. Drop your treble approach to life. Add a merciless focus on fundamentals. This will create happy intestines and put a pop gleam on your lip."

An authoritarian streak rose through the doctor's throat, momentarily visiting the Zany brain. "Martha, you are very wise."

She handed him a cookie. "Hammer it freely," she continued. "Mix toes with thighs, add digression, then pour. Bowels will sing, and digestion will improve."

"I want singing bowels."

"Of course," she added matter-of-factly. Returning to the kitchen, she stirred the porridge, and called back, "Everyone does. Schopenhauer, in *Der Vorschlag auf Wiedersehen An-schlutz Vergangenheit mit Schnitzel Laufen,* says bass sounds are one of the few universals left in this tainted, forgettable world."

After breakfast, Zany lay down on his front lawn and waited for his digestive juices to work their wonders. He dozed, re-laxed, and soon fell asleep.

Attila appeared before him in a dream. Standing high on the branch of a tree to his right, his son rained twisted etymolo-gies upon his prostrate father. "Decadence is deca-dance in dis-guise—dance of the ten! Time to get up! Thank your pagan gods. Misery has created a new routine for you. Rise and ride, Father. Stretch your weary limbs. Let Deca Dance embrace you! Handed down by Moses himself. Here on Mt. Ararat, I have discovered that the Hebrew leader took a two-year break from Exodus to search for the ancient ark. In his spare time, he learned that, aside from knowing the origin of all languages, Noah had consulted with his animals to understand the hidden potential and secret choreographic meaning of Deca-Dance. Its sculptural movements cure emptiness, depression, and insomnia. By creating a vacuum in your brain, it releases space for higher learning to enter. Father, here is my plea: Grab its purposeless form! Cling to its emptiness! A new door will open, and through its doorway will rush rising hopes, dreams, and a *new life!*"

Attila vanished. Zany rubbed his eyes as he woke. Rising, he looked around his lawn, fixed his eyes on the growing maple tree shading his front steps, and patiently watched it grow. An hour later, confidant in his vision, he announced with renewed energy: "My first step is to declare *I will succeed!*"

He found Martha in the kitchen, preparing a stew. He took her hand, rubbed her palm, gazed deeply into her eyes, and said, "Martha, I am planning for success."

"Let go of me. I'm busy." She pushed him away. ". . . Wait a minute. What did you just say?"

"I'm planning for success!"

The cook put down her ladle. "Even though you gave thousands of concerts, Dr. Zany, you always walked on glass, slipped on ice, and twisted in the wind. *Now* you say you are giving up these old loser thoughts? Why change now? What has happened to you?" She peppered her stew, tasted it, spat it out in disgust, and dumped it into the garbage can.

As they spoke, St. James and Kohan entered the living room for a morning conference. St. James sat down in Zany's armchair, pulled out his pipe, lit his tobacco, and inhaled with deep pleasure. Zany left the kitchen to sit down with them. Having overheard the conversation in the kitchen, The Apostle blew out a circle of smoke and said, "Zoltan, I didn't realize you were such an optimist."

Kohan was munching on a cookie. "Shamans are natural optimists."

A sparrow had flown into the house through the bathroom window. Martha stamped her foot, opened the kitchen door, and when the sparrow flew out, exclaimed, "Zany is *not* a shaman."

"He's not Mongolian either," St. James answered.

"The Mongolian shaman monopoly was broken years ago," Genghis offered. "Individual entrepreneurship is now the rule. In fact, only a few reside in Ulan Bator. The others are too busy spreading their teaching throughout the world. These days a shaman can come from anywhere—Mongolia, Turkey, Hawaii,

Syria, Argentina, New Jersey. Although human birth is their usual creation venue, some *have* been known to rise from rocks, rivers, trees, and sod as well."

St. James laughed. "Zany, a shaman! What a joke!"

"One never knows who a shaman might be," said Genghis. "Rebirth occurs in strange ways. Let's see how he plays the violin now."

Martha stood by the bathroom door. "Zany a shaman," she wondered. "Is it possible? Is that why Attila went to Turkey? Part of a secret cosmic plan?"

"Maybe," said St. James. "After all, he is traveling with the notorious Isaac 'Cookie' Mashugi. Some say the professor is an undercover linguistic agent working for the Mossad; others claim the man is trying to de-construct the world through etymology."

"Utter rubbish," Zany protested. "False accusations. All disproved three years ago in the *Hindermatterhausenpliederhof Papers* of Ludwig von Wittgenstein."

Suddenly, the spirit of Attila again appeared as freckles of thought in Zany's mind.

His son spoke, his nebulous form constantly shifting its virtual shape. "Father, all is well here. After my flight landed in Istanbul, Cookie and I headed for Ararat. Our trek up the mountain was picturesque and thrilling. Many wild animals said hello, including a fox, a rabbit, and a wild donkey that kicked Mashugi when he mispronounced a Hittite word. Best of all, I think we found Noah's Ark! The discovery made me feel so great, I started my own meditation practice. Inspired by the Sadhus of India, I stood on my right leg for ten days, facing the Ark. In the process, I discovered an untapped love of travel. It happened the minute I stepped on my left leg again when *I saw stars!* Isaac said a lack of circulation had caused the vision, but I knew it was a signal, the call for deeper knowledge of travel. Among those stars I spied planets, distant galaxies, whole universes! All were ready to be discovered by humankind. I realized *I* could show them the way, and, through counseling and consultation, lead them to a higher reality. When my circulation returned, I had a new entrepreneurial idea: Start my own company, the Attila Tour Consultation and Counseling Service (ATCCS).

"After doing his own meditation practice, standing on his left leg for three hours, *Cookie* said he wanted to join my company as president, but I said that's my job. So he took the position of Etymology Director. How about you? Since you're no longer in your armchair, would you like to be part of this venture?

"Isaac and I continue our search for the primal word, the first utterance of mankind. We'll also plan to combine our etymological research with travel and create a travel subsidiary to our counseling service (ATCCS). Our specialty will be trekking—leading hikes up Mount Ararat. We'll include a visit to Noah's ark.

"I may also change my name to Attila Peripateticus.

"Father, what do you think about all this?"

Zany emerged from his telepathic trance, told his partners about the Attila dream visit, and, in a spasm of near-visionary discourse, revealed plans for his own future and the long-term goals of their company.

St. James sucked deeply on his pipe. "You've been doing heavyweight thinking."

Kohan's eyes danced with hopes. "Maybe we'll even visit Mongolia!"

Three days later, Dr. Zany packed his violin, warm clothes, extra socks, hiking boots, his favorite toothbrush, and *Turkish History from Neolithic to Ottoman Times,* by Ozkok Beyaltun. Rushing out the front door, he mumbled a quick goodbye to Martha, jumped in a taxi, headed for the airport, and boarded a 7:30 p.m. flight on Turkish Airline flight to Istanbul.

28

CONVERSATIONS ON MOUNT ARARAT

IN ISTANBUL, ZANY PASSED through airport security and boarded a Yollari Airline flight to Van in Eastern Turkey.

When he reached the Van airport, he checked his watch and disembarked. Midnight. Not a soul in sight. Totally deserted. He listened with satisfaction to the silence surrounding him. Peace reigned. The bright white of the Grande Dipperette, sister of the Big Dipper, had risen high in the Turkish sky.

Outside the airport, he found a taxi driver sleeping in his cab, woke him, placed himself and his luggage in the back seat, said, "Askerbejad Hotel, *lutfin*," and, twenty minutes later, mounted the wooden stairs of the one-star hotel to his room, consisting of a straw mattress, squat toilet, and combo shower and bathroom. He slept for fourteen hours.

The next day, walking through the colorful streets of Van, he purchased a Turkish cushion from an Armenian vendor whose quick "Shnoorhagulatzion" stunned Zany's post-flight, cochlear- challenged inner ear.

"Where did you find such a word?" he asked the musta-chioed salesman with a blue, green, and purple yellow-square-patterned rug draped across his shoulders. The Armenian leaned to the right, tilted his head to reflect a beam of sunlight from his eyeglasses, and looked straight into Zany's eyes. "It means 'Thank you.'"

Zany blinked protectively as he considered the musical significance of this "schnoor" sound. When he opened his eyes again, the salesman had disappeared.

The violinist had already decided the write a symphony upon Turkish and Armenian themes. Its working title, *Mount Ararat Descent Number One,* had appeared to him two weeks before, when he imagined a trek down Ararat after an earthquake and mud slides had destroyed his walking path. During this waking dream, he had slid forty feet down the mountain, ending up in a canyon underneath a fallen pine tree. "A sign from Above," he'd concluded. As the fantasy continued, he'd grabbed a pine needle, and, using leaf ink, scribbled the first symphonic notes on the igneous rock to his right. Or was it metamorphic? As the rock slide careened down the hill, pieces of broken balsa wood had whipped past his head, landing near a cave to his left. Zany had sensed they came from Noah's ark. At that moment, the symphonic title had leaped hard and strong into his head.

"Yes, I'll use the 'schnoor' in my prelude or in the Overture," he concluded.

After another night's rest in Van, Zany felt ready to travel. Next morning, he took a bus to the foot of Ararat, where he met Attila. The lad's shoulders seemed to have grown broader; he was wearing archaeological dungarees with patches of Hittite cuneiform writing; his cheeks shone with the vibrant hope of future etymological discoveries. "Attila, you're looking healthy and strong," the doctor exclaimed, giving his son a giant bear hug.

Attila stepped back, looked at his father's wide mustache, well-shaved face, neatly combed hair, and freshly pressed pants. "You're looking fit, too," he said. "I sense your armchair sitting days are finished."

"Indeed, they are. My mind is ready to compose. My body is ready to roll." Zany reached into his valise and pulled out the preliminary sketches for his new Turkish symphony. "Take a look at this." He spread the seven-page manuscript on the ground.

Attila perused it quickly. Carrying his AK-47 for protection against trees and wandering Babylonian terrorists, he aimed it at the treble clef on page one. "Let me add a few notes," he said.

"Treble or bass clef?" his father asked.

Attila's eyes blazed with fire. "All clefs are fair game," he cried, discharging a burst of machine gun fire into the dormant manuscript.

Fully satisfied his father's work had been cleansed of impurities, Attila shouldered his weapon. A new authority filled his voice. "We're ready to move on."

Zany examined the bullet holes and collected his newly edited Turkish symphony from the sidewalk. "Scoring it for drum and trumpet will work better. I'll subtitle it 'Noah's Overture.'"

"Father, as I shot, did you notice pieces of wood flying past? I believe they were remnants of Noah's Ark."

"Could be. I smell the animals."

"You do? I'm so glad! We're close to discovery. Mashugi will be ecstatic."

Father and son soon began a two-day trek to base camp. Zany tweaked his five-day growth of beard and plucked a feather from his eyebrow. Birds flying overhead looked gray. That evening, beacons of light shone from distant Van. The far-sighted adventurer could even see the city of Kirkuk in Iraq.

Next morning, the snowy peaks of Mt. Ararat appeared in the distance. Attila shouted, "Father! Wake-up time. Wonder of wonders! I saw another piece of Ark flying past. Wow!" His eyes gleamed as stamped on the ground; Ercek clumps of dirt fell from his shoes. Suddenly, they heard the roar of an avalanche.

"Too much kicking!" said Zany, who turned over and went back to sleep.

He awoke an hour later. "Attila, my favorite and only son," he said, "your morning words amaze me. Have you accidently shot off your fourth toe? Could it be the rat-tat-tat of your AK-47 has finally penetrated your etymologically engorged head? I never heard you speak of joy before, and certainly not of *wonders.*"

Attila prepared coffee. While rolling up his sleeping bag and stirring the pot, he answered, "Yes, Father. Last night a surge of electrified moonbeams jolted my body. I'm a new man today!"

Zany shook his head in disbelief. "If this is true, it took Turkey to do it. I feel jubilant about this victory! At last I've beaten your mother in the happy-son game!"

Attila put his hand gently on his father's knee. "My happiest feeling will come when we stand before Noah's Ark, exhausted and triumphant! Ah, I sense Mashugi is ready. I can hear his unconscious panting. Let's move on. Our search continues. Secretly and in silence, The Word and Ark are waiting!"

29

ARCHAEOLOGY

THE FOLLOWING DAY, FATHER and son were standing under a blue sky in brilliant sunlight, facing the distant peak of Mount Ararat. Morning dew dabbed their cheeks. Attila was explaining, "According to Mashugi's research, Noah suffered from flu. His wife, Mary Madagascar, had many small animals under her skein."

Zany looked at his son, shook his head, and sighed. "My dear Attila, I know my bible. There is no record of her name."

"Mashugi does not work with *records*. Nor does he care much for physical evidence. Facts never get in his way. The man uses only intuition."

"You mean he never *read* the bible? Not even the Old Testament?"

"He *used* to read. But last May Cookie gave up reading and upgraded his research technique by. . .well, actually, by gazing at stars."

"Mary Madagascar, eh?" Zany reached into memory; childhood Torah studies emerged in his cerebellum; soon they flooded his mind. "The midrash in Bereshit Rabba 23:3 fills this void," he observed. "Remember Genesis 4.22, where Tuval Kain's sister was Na'amah? Rabbi Abba bar Kohanah said Na'amah was the wife of Noah. Why was she called Na'amah, 'the pleasant one'? Were her deeds really so pleasing? Mashugi'd better watch his step. As a violinist, I know this woman beat false rhythms on the drum to accompany her idolatry."

"Oh, shut up, Father. Don't bore me with details and suppositions. What do you know about the bible, anyway?"

"More than you," Zany retorted. "In fact, I also know I can help in your *quest*. Like Mashugi, I too work with intuition. But my mentor, Mother Zany, also believed in facts."

"What did she know about the ark?"

"Not much. But she could easily find lost shoes, coats, and shirts in cluttered closets. She once even found a thimble and thread her grandmother had used. What is archaeological research but that?"

"You have a point there," Attila admitted. A hint of pride shone in the machine gunner's eyes as he glanced at the clear Turkish sky. "I'm glad to hear intuition is part of our family tradition."

A blank look emptied Zany's face. Suddenly, he whirled, lurched right, and fell to the ground.

Attila looked amused. He had seen this kind of "passion collapse" many times in the past. He surmised that father had fallen into his horizontal ecstasy position, the awe-and-wonder slide. Was this one an arpeggio stupor derived from the etymological root of the Latin *stupor,* meaning "wonder?" In so doing, was he assuming his place next to Friedrich II von Hohenstaufer, twelfth-century genius king and ruler of Sicily, initiator of its medieval golden age, known to the world as *Stupor*

Mundo? Or this time, was it something different? Could father actually be ill?

"Is this one a heart attack?" Attila queried.

Zany opened his eyes, rolled them counterclockwise, slid beneath a sycamore tree, folded his legs in full lotus, and leaned against the trunk. He sat quietly in deep meditation. Leaves tinted autumnal gold shaded his tanned, deeply wrinkled, sunspotted head.

Four hours later, he reopened his eyes. Attila was sitting patiently in front of him. Zany stared at his son, then explained, "Something just happened in my mind. I heard a giant *click*. Then a terrifying ball of fire rolled down from the peak of Mount Ararat. It gained speed as it approached me. When you said 'Mashugi,' the ball of fire struck me in the chest. My heart exploded."

Attila knew about these things. "Sounds like your usual apocalyptic vision coming straight out of St. John's cave in Patmos. A volcano attack. Maybe that island is erupting again. Or this time it might be violin *Revelations* exiting from *your* cave."

Zany waved off the idea. "This click has nothing to do with Patmos. I hate islands. They smell of isolation and death—except perhaps for Long Island, which has traffic jams to keep you company. I'm a mountain man. I thrive on heights."

"Strange you should faint before Mount Ararat. Well, maybe not *so* strange—for a Zany. These falls are part of our family history. I remember your bedtime stories. But why did you insist that my sister Hilda sit in on them?"

"You never had a sister."

"You still deny her existence! But don't you remember when Mother let her sleep in the closet?"

"What are you talking about? Too much Turkish sun has fried your brain."

"All right, never mind Hilda. Go on. Tell me what just happened."

Zany stamped his foot. "I shall not!"

"Father, old memories are coming up." Attila adopted a softer, more psychologically responsive tone. "Could this relate to your childhood trip to Greece? You told me that, when you were nine, Grandpa Zany taught you religion in Thessaly. Remember? How he drove you to the cliff monasteries of Meteora? He promised to teach you flight by throwing you off a cliff."

Zany put his head back, trying to recall a tasty Kalambaka souvlaki. "Attila, I never knew you possessed such acumen. I'm impressed. Time spent with Mashugi has sharpened your brain." He reflected another moment. "Aha, now I recall! When Grandpa Zany tried pushing me off the Varlaam Monastery cliff, I *did* learn to fly! I flew straight into the bathroom and locked the door. I stayed in that toilet for three days. When I finally opened the door, Grandpa Zany was standing in front of it. He smiled wisely beneath his mustache, said something about the trinity and the significance of the number three as key to personal and spiritual transfiguration. Then he gave me a big hug and took me home."

"There's a monastery in Trabzon on the Black Sea coast, too," said Attila. "Perhaps we should go there. Black Sea waters are very calming."

"No, Mt. Ararat is fine. I like the fresh air. Besides, I don't need a monastery anymore. The monks told me the monastery is within. I believe them. Now I'm happy wherever I am."

3⚙

A TOUCH OF HAPPINESS

THE TURKISH SUN SAT high in the sky. A fresh breeze blew from the East. Attila sat again before his father, listening, his AK-47 resting lightly in his lap. "You can't beat happiness," he agreed. "But, Father, aside from happiness, how will violin playing help our search for Noah's Ark and man's original Ur-word?"

"That's easy," Zany answered. "Violin and Word are one."

"That's very mystical. Also dangerous."

"Dangerous? Why?" Zany paused before brushing the concept aside with a wave of his hand. "Never mind. No need to explain. Back to my happiness: How do I know that violin, or music, and Word are one? Well, in order to experience this truth, travel inward. You'll be treading a solo path to the original sound. Everyone can find it. But it's hidden inside you. On this voyage, you often recall infant grunts, screams, wails, cries, laughs, and gurgles; you remember mother as 'one who knows.' But of course, she doesn't know either. It's a personal quest. Only you can know. Your goal is to relive ancient moments, visit pre-womb times, archaic episodes. Once you learn to familiarize yourself with your own inner Ur-music, you'll easily find any future Ur-sounds. As for Noah's Ark, listen to the animal noises as they come out two-by-two, hear their grunts, cries, belches. Listen to Noah himself and the sounds of his family. All this makes Ur-music easier to hear. Keep following this pattern. You'll see how it works. It's a gradual process. But after much practice and exploration, one day, in sudden revelation, the Ur- sound will be heard, and the All will be yours!"

"So that's how it's done."

"Exactly." Zany exhaled. "It's an experiment of one. You are an experiment of one. Each person must find their own unique Aural Path. Although they may benefit from inspirational help, it is alone, in the privacy of their own mind, they hear the world's first sound."

"Pop, you amaze me. How did you figure all this out?"

"Years of violin practice, Beethoven and Bruch violin concertos. Hours in the kitchen with Martha also helped."

"The Zen of Zany," Attila exclaimed with admiration. "Fifteen years ago, you built a base of violin fans. You told me they followed the Zany/Beethoven Way. I called you arrogant and self-serving. You answered, 'Maybe.' Then 'But maybe not.' A moment later, you added, 'The Way is not about self-worship. It's about mitzvahs and igniting sparks.'

"I loved it! You created a warm glow: *The Zany moment.* But the question remains: How to achieve it? Father, can such a moment be defined, re-created by others? Or is it a solitary, personal thing?"

"Attila, what excellent questions!" Zany looked pleased. He smiled with pleasure, then hesitated. ". . .I feel a strange malaise coming on."

"Could the problem be that everything is all right?"

Zany shook his head. "You silly ward of the state. Hasn't central government taught you anything? What happened to your capitalism and entrepreneurial lessons?"

"Books in English are hard to find here. I've got nothing to read except *Embrace Communism* by Neptune Cleopatra. She believes in—"

"What kind of answer is that? What would your mother say?"

"Embrace Marxism."

"You're diving into oblivion again, skidding off track. Mama Zany never said that. She believed in reptilian rule. Frogs forever! Hop about! Those were her mottos. Reptilarian collectivist philosophies, and tadpole accumulation, were only considered when things got tough."

Zany unlaced his shoes. A sudden foot-freedom desire had overtaken him. "I too have been veering off course. Let my toes point the way. Attila, your Word and Ur-sound search is a worthy one. Keep searching. Onward, sideward, and upward. I'm with you even when I'm not. But with or without me, the everlasting sound search continues." The barefoot Zany jumped to his feet and shouted. "Where is Mashugi? Time to go! Let's map out our plans."

"Finally! I'm so happy about this decision. Father, your violin brain will be an asset."

"Assets are good. So are liabilities. I plan to be both."

"Good, good."

"Violin playing teaches us that the search for the ultimate sound starts at the podiatric bottom. Embrace sole and heel! Though vibrating and interpreted in the head, the Ur sound begins in the foot."

31

ISAAC "COOKIE" MASHUGI

NEW PURPOSE COURSED THROUGH Zany's veins. He felt like one of the boys, equal in age, stature, mental agility, physical stamina, and vision to the ever-shooting, ever-searching, AK-47 Attila. Father and son were finally united on their quest. Up ahead lay the snow-capped peaks of Mount Ararat. They hiked along a steep mountain trail, heading to base camp, Camp Mashugi.

Passing brooks, rocks, pines, glades, and strands of Ararat grasses, they arrived in a field surrounded by apple trees. Birds sang; a vulture was siting in a branch to the right. Or was it an eagle? Attila spied Mashugi's cellophane-and-canvas tent up ahead. "There it is!" he shouted, charging forward. In a few moments, breathless and panting, they were standing before the tent door flap.

Isaac Mashugi came to the door—short, stocky, muscular, his dancing blue eyes mirroring his jiggling stomach.

Zany saluted him. "Your soldiers are ready!" he cried. "Your generals, too. Our feet are greased and itch to patrol!"

Mashugi looked at the doctor and immediately understood

the soul mate strangeness standing before him. Enlightened by instant rapport, he replied in a Germano/Hebraic/Babylonio/ Russo/Arabic/ French, hypo-Mongolian, subto-Altaic/ Tungusic/Azeri/ Turko-Kazakhstani/Korean, and Persian accent, "The undrum is in the conundrum."

"Come off it, Cookie," snapped Attila. "Some *comprehensibility* for guests. This is my father."

"I sensed that," Mashugi boomed, his baritone voice now fully engaged. Adopting a Napoleonic pose, he offered a calloused hand to Zany. "Glad to meet you, father of Attila." The archaeologist bowed, removed his ten-gallon cowboy yarmulka, and dramatically swept it across the ground. "Excuse the display of verbal and mental gymnastics." he apologized. "When I meet a new member of the human species, I descend deep into the dark mental side to find their treatment. Or rather, a notion of how I might treat them. It's a mysterious, twisted place, and I sometimes get lost on my way out."

"Totally understandable," Zany responded. "I used to go there myself. But three years ago, I had my cleaning woman sweep and mop the place, wash the windows, and make it lighter. Since then, I've had no problem."

Mashugi looked impressed. "Good idea. I might try that someday," he said. Both doctors shook hands.

"Your son says yours is a *musical* mind." the archeologist affirmed.

"It is," Zany replied. "But musical, intellectual, archeological, or contemporary, in the upper reaches all mentalities respond to the same subtle vibrations. Both Beethoven and Hegel had giant minds. Only Ludwig knew how to play the piano."

"Ah, you're a wise farter," Mashugi declared.

"*Father* is the word. Mr. Mashugi, I notice you have a deep, rich voice, very musical. Nothing to be ashamed of there."

"*Doctor* Mashugi." the archaeologist insisted. "Thank you, Mr. Zany—"

"*Doctor* Zany."

"Aha."

"Zoltan for you."

"Cookie here. Well, Zoltan, *toda raba*. My voice, although not musical, is nevertheless, deep. It comes from my genealogical *shoresh*, or family root. When my mother, Malka Mashugi, was a child in Lithuania, she dreamed of becoming an opera singer. My father, Abraham, also the town rabbi, forbade it. He had developed an original interpretation of Orthodoxy. 'In Noadic tradition,' he claimed, 'chanting is only for men. Women, however, are allowed to sing while they cook.' As the ninth male child, my mother hoped that I would carry on her vocal tradition. Although I did not learn her operatic skills, I did inherit her vocal cords, along with an enjoyment of flattery."

Zany straightened to attention. "Well, whatever history you have, I'm at your service."

Mashugi glanced at Zany's feet, twisted his lips with concern. He bent to examine the violinist's sole. "You suffer from Greek feet."

"Greek feet? I never heard of that."

"It's a common podiatric ailment—the opposite of Turkish feet. I suggest rest."

Zany shook his head. "Rest? I hate rest. Is it necessary? Besides, searching for the Word will energize me."

A childhood memory of Mother Zany beating a carpet on the clothesline flashed through his mind. She had beaten that rug with a stick, shouting, "Die, you! Die!" before calling the sun to finish the job. Her method had worked every time. Rugs had responded by getting clean very quickly. No hesitation there. "Jump right in" was her motto.

"Personally, I'd like to jump right in," Zany added. "It saves time."

Mashugi had no reply. But the cosmos did. The weather suddenly turned nasty. Hailstones began to fall. "Damn!" cursed Zany. "How discouraging. Doesn't He ever give up? I thought I'd finally been released, that I was now free to roam with mammoths, sing with crocodiles, feast with turtles, and run laps with reindeer!"

Hurricane winds were soon bending trees, sending leaves and twigs whizzing through the air, and scattering pebbles along the road. Nearby oak branches rubbed together. Zany's heard them laugh. "Zany," they cackled, "You'll *never be free!* Once, long ago, you believed in liberty. Ha! How naive. Your reward is not freedom, but the gift of perpetual slavery! Any true artist knows that. But evidently, though concertizing throughout the world, you never reached artistic maturity. Liberty is a disease. Your answer is: *Never* more freedom. *Always* more slavery! As one of your former philosophical heroes, the French philosopher Jean-Paul Sartless said, 'The free man is one who is free to *choose* his form of slavery.' You once loved that phrase. Somehow, breathing the rarified air of Mount Ararat has made you forget."

Zany bent his head. "You're right," he sighed, voice heavy with shame. "I *have* forgotten. Sitting so much has diluted my brain. An armchair year, followed by this wild trip to Turkey, have caused old values to slip into the sewer. Thank you, wise Druid trees. You reminded my of my true self and cause. Although I find physical slavery offensive, mental slavery is within my capacity. Especially a slavery *I choose.* Indeed, I've chained myself to violin practice; I spend hours every day bound by and embracing its discipline. Also I realize, that, in the long run, such slavery creates barrels of fun. I remember using all my strength for days as I struggled with technical difficulties. Finally, I'd conquer them! When that happened, I'd jump up, race out of my room, charge out of the house, and run down the street shouting, laughing, dancing, and waving my hands in wild abandon. *Victory!*"

The trees rustled in agreement. "Now you're starting to get it, Zany," they laughed. "You remember. As our Druid sister, Third Tree says, 'Remembrance is future in reverse.'"

"She's a wise tree," Zany acknowledged.

"Thank you, Herr Zany."

"You're welcome. Last question, my Druids."

"Yes?"

"Why do all of you speak German?"

32

THE TREK BEGINS

WHERE IS NOAH'S ARK? *Where—and what—is the Word?* Zany woke from his biblical revery with these questions.

Throwing off his blankets, he rose from his bed, drew open the camping tent flaps, and inhaled the fresh mountain air. Mashugi and Attila lay under brown army blankets near him, still snoring.

What lay ahead and behind? Where do "ahead" and "behind" meet? What language would their twisted search-and-discovery process use? Would knowing the Urword help?

"I'm packed and ready to go!"

Attila and Mashugi slept on, dreaming possible answers to these questions. Zany, however, wide awake, violin fingers and body parts flushed with excitement, paced the floor space between the sleeping archaeologists.

Finally, he knelt to shake them.

"Let's go, let's go!" he insisted.

Attila was first to stir.

"Father, first we have to pack."

Zany patted his knapsack. "I've got my sandwich."

"We'll need more than that." Attila rolled to his side, cleared his throat, and pushed himself into standing position. "Wake Mashugi. He knows about packing for linguistic treks."

Three hours later, saddled with goods and provisions, prepared for their trek up the morning mountain, they began working their way through the snow.

"It will soon be time for snowshoes," Mashugi advised.

The Noadic team ploughed on, passing a waterfall with icicles hanging from the rocks.

"Why is playing violin in front of audiences more difficult than playing alone?" Attila panted.

"I'm beginning to ask the same question," Zany replied, turning toward his son. "*I'm* looking, too. Maybe that's why I'm climbing Mount Ararat. I've got unanswered questions. The violinist Vladimir Poofman, when asked how he dealt with his concert audiences, answered, 'I don't *mind* if they listen.'"

Zany reached into his knapsack, pulled out his sandwich, and took a bite.

Attila reached over. "I'm hungry. Give me some, too."

"Be quiet!" snorted Mashugi from the slope above them. "Ten more minutes before you touch a mouthful."

The climb up Mount Ararat possessed, for Zany, striking similarities to a violin ascent on the fingerboard, an upward climb of scale practice. Finger after finger, pound after fleshy pound, ascending a ladder of sound, from C to C, or A to A, or whatever the instrumental calibrations happened to be, this reptilian digital climb began with every Zany morning warm-up: Scales followed by arpeggios. But for the past two years, in semi-retirement, or rather, as Attila called it, "retardment," he had practiced nothing. Oh, there had been scattered moments up the fingerboard, a few minutes of bowing, but otherwise nothing.

Every ascending scale must descend. And vice versa. But living permanently in a stationary chord, a place of rests with no scales at all, could never satisfy Zany's appetites. Would he rediscover this ancient wisdom on the mountain top? He needed to return to New Jersey with a new attitude, one enabling him to fulfill a life beyond his New Jersey armchair?

What was a "scale?" What did it really mean? What was the kabalistic essence of its nature? As Jacob discovered in his bible dream, scales are ladders to heaven; angels run up and down its rungs, bringing messages from the Divine Source. Thus, playing scales had a transcendent purpose. Hidden meaning existed in each pattern.

Indeed, each artist was a secret bhodisattva. Riding on wings of ascending notes, they climb to heaven, to drink of celestial joy. Then, instead of remaining in heaven's serene eternal embrace, they *choose* return to the material realm below. With compassion, love, and desire to heal, they embrace the wounded world. In this lower land of chaos and pain, they teach their secret of bubbling laughter. Riding on descending notes, they offer Magnificence to lost, lonely, smoke-infested searchers, the frantic, unilluminated inhabitants of the Earth.

Zany's mind was cooking. He liked what he was thinking.

Along with his sandwich, he had packed a violin A string in his knapsack—440 vibrations per second. A sudden desire to play violin gripped his being.

What a strange, familiar, and wonderful feeling it was. Could this be why he had come to Turkey? What was the higher purpose of trekking? Why climb Mount Ararat? What did a mountain symbolize and *express?*

In his famous *Concert of the Breaking Strings*, Paganini had broken one string after another. Finally, only one string had been left. Nevertheless, the concert had not stopped. The master continued playing brilliantly on that string. Evidently, one string was enough. Well, if one string was enough for Paganini, how about no strings for Zany? A no-string player giving a no-string concert—it fired the violinist's imagination.

Zany had a sudden flashback to childhood and his mother's negative comments, not only about early violin lessons, but about her son's inferior dishwashing techniques and room-cleaning habits. Could he ever eradicate that inferiority complex from his sensitive, childlike heart?

And, while Zany was at it, what was this "Word" that Mashugi and Attila incessantly talked about? Were there surprises on Mount Ararat?

The grade got steeper. Zany looked back. "How's it going, Attila?" he gasped.

"I'm still visiting the Universal Self."

Zany shook his son. "*Dump* that Indian philosophy and Universal Self stuff."

"Why? You're so philosophical this morning, Father. Is it the high altitude and mountain air? I've never heard such thoughts coming out of your head."

"You're right," Zany admitted. "They *are* strange. I wonder what they mean?"

"Maybe we'll find answers in the Word," answered Attila.

33

ENTREPRENEUR IN TURKISH MODE

THEY PASSED THROUGH KARAKOSEKET, a village hanging on the edge of a cliff, hovering over a river and underneath a cloud. As Zany ambled down the street, a tall, broad-shouldered man approached them. Wearing his Anatolian scarf, wide Konya parchese pants, and nylon wolf shorts from which emerged immense gastrocnemius muscles, he tried grabbing Zany by the foot. The swift violinist side-stepped him with a Beethovenian quartet-and-concerto *plie*. The giant plunged past, falling head first onto a sewer pipe. He rose slowly, dusted himself off, and extended a wide, fat hand.

"Dear sir, welcome to our village." The man's deep bass voice purred in humble tones. "We are a suburb of Agri, or Karakose. Our city, so high and mighty here in the highlands of eastern Turkey, lies 5,380 feet above sea level. Wonderful real estate values extended from valleys to mountain peaks. Marvelous views of the Murat River, a tributary of the Euphrates, abound. Nearby Karakose does a lively trade in livestock and livestock products. Our village, so near the main highway from Turkey to Iran, also offers ample travel opportunities.

"But let me personalize my offering. I am Selim Altun Tessekur Ederimchik, head of the town council. In English, I am known as Thank-You Man. My entrepreneurial father, Ahmed Harquile Gomer Sinez Akaharmon Tessekur Ederimchik, was a famous real estate agent in Eastern Turkey. I learned at his feet—and he passed his skills on to me. Would you care to purchase some land? Perhaps a farm, a town dwelling, a river, a fountain, a carpet factory, a field, a rocky escarpment, meadow, or cave? Since abandonment of the underground city of Kayaresi, westward movements of its inhabitants, fall of Constantinople, and collapse of the Byzantine Empire in 1453, we have had many caves for sale."

Dr. Zany considered the proposal as he looked quizzically at the real estate entrepreneur. "I like caves," he finally said. "I'm looking for a place to retire, or at least rest and meditate for a few decades. I have become world weary. Would you have something for me?"

Ahmed's eyes brightened. "Oh, yes, indeed, Mr. . . . ?"

"Zany is the name."

"Ah, yes Mr. Chaney."

"Zany."

"Djeny."

"Zany."

"Zany." Zany nodded. Ahmed looked pleased. "Yes, Mr. Zany, we have many caves to fit your liking. Would this be only for sitting? Or would you like standing as well?"

"I need a place where I can play violin as well as read, write, and meditate."

"With sunlit entrance? Or do prefer a lugubrious dimness, excellent for meditation, or funereal darkness, the preferred lighting for long-term sleep?"

"I prefer a cave in which I can go forward, backward, and roundabout."

"By 'forward', do you mean straight into the future?"

"Exactly."

"By 'backward', do you mean to explore your past?"

"Indeed."

"By roundabout, do you mean not walking around in socks but rather circumlocution based on the Peripatetic School of Aristotelian philosophy?"

"Perfect!"

Ahmed's voice rose in excitement. "I have just the cave for you! Its entrance faces the future! If you exit through the back and bear right, you'll go directly into the past! If you bear left, you'll visit ancient, mythological domains, your old neighborhood, forgotten parts of your family, and more. If you are truly adventurous, you can even go straight to Hades!"

"You mean I could visit my personal and historic ancestors?"

"Absolutely. Your future family and upcoming events, too." A wild radiant kind of light filled Ahmed's eyes as his excitement rose. "*Evet.* This cave is perfect for the living and the dead."

"How much?"

Ahmed thought for a long sales moment. "Considering that you are my friend," he said, "and such a wonderful man, I shall make a special price of four trillion lira."

"That's a bit excessive."

"Ah, my friend, but once you see it, you will realize what a bargain I offer."

"Can you do any better?"

"No!" Ahmed shook his head vigorously. "I love the property too much. I cannot part with it for one lira less."

"Sorry to hear that." Zany turned to leave.

Ahmed grabbed his arm. "Such a wonderful property! But, well, for you my friend, I can do something special. Since it is June and you are my first customer of the day, for good luck, I will offer you this stellar property for a mere 3.8 trillion lira."

Zany counted the zeros. "That's only 200 billion less. Can't you make a better offer?"

Ahmed took Zany by the arm. Guiding him gently but forcefully, he said, "Come into my real estate shop. We'll talk."

The two men spent the remaining hours of the day together. By late afternoon, Zany had said, "2 million."

Ahmed countered with: "3 ½."

"2.2."

"3.4."

Ahmed paused, held his breath, and rose. "Time to take our traditional break from bargaining. Would you care to read, or relax under an apple shade tree? Mr. Zany, aside from laboring in orchards and real estate, I am also an author. I have written many best sellers, as well as books that remain in *my* cellars."

"Is that right?" Zany was impressed. "Would I like your books?"

"Of course."

"Good. I love reading. My eager mind eats up volumes. I used to read all day long during my armchair sabbatical back in the States."

Ahmed's eyes shone. "Ah, an eager verbal participant."

"Yes, in fact, my son and I, along with his archaeologist colleague, are in Turkey exploring Mt. Ararat on a verbal search. They are looking for the Ur Word. You wouldn't happen to know where it is?

"The Ur Word? Do you mean the word in all real estate contracts of Selim Bajarofelimkarokoy?"

"I'm not sure."

"Ah! The Word of. . . ? " Ahmed pointed his thumb upward.

"Exactly. It's really a sound." Zany shoved a pinky in his ear to clean out some wax. "That's why I, a violinist, came along to help. The Word might be such a subtle vibration they'd miss it, even if it sounded right next to them."

"True, they *could* miss it. Where do they expect to find this sound?

"Mashugi, the archaeologist, believes it is located in Noah's Ark. They hope to find remnants near the top of Mt. Ararat."

Ahmed laughed softly and laid a hand on Zany's shoulder. "My old friend," he counseled in wise, paternal manner, "I'm in real estate. Why should your son and his friend waste their precious time trekking? I know where this 'Noah's Ark' is."

"You do?

"Of course. After you purchase your cave, I could lead you there."

"*The* Noah's Ark?"

"Any ark you like. After all, I'm in real estate."

"2.5," Zany offered.

"Never! It must be 2.95."

"You said you are an author?" Zany asked. "What kind of books do you write?"

"Good question." Ahmed patted his stomach with his left hand and wiped his mouth with his right. "My books are philosophic: They contain hidden meanings, secret philosophies, mysteries of the universe. They begin where Sufi writing ends. Many years ago, I worked as a whirling dervish in Konya and Istanbul. We practiced turning for hours, spinning and spinning as we moving in and out of deep meditation. As we whirled, we entered a higher sphere, a land of deep wisdom, knowledge, and learning. Your Mashugi friend may already know that the Indo- Iranian word *dervish* is etymologically related to the English word *door*. By whirling, the dervish opens the door to heaven."

"Really? I didn't know that."

"2.95."

"2.4." Zany countered.

"2.75," Ahmed responded.

"2.5."

"2.65."

Ahmed leaned back in his chair. "It's true," he said. "I learned the etymology of 'dervish' from Aslan Akjaharmon while he helped my father open up his first Grand Minaret Restaurant in Istanbul. A lion of a man. I worked there for three years, making lamb, veal, chicken, spinach-and-cauliflower, and beef- and-sausage kekbabs. Aslan counseled me on mysteries of food and the universe. It inspired me to create my culinary and literary masterpiece, the mystico-philosophical treatise, *Al Shish Kebabka*. While I penned it during two intense weeks of creative passion, I contracted kebab *fever*."

"That's *so* interesting!"

"2 million 6."

"Sold."

The two men shook hands. Zany took a sip of tea, picked up his map and contract, and said goodbye to Ahmed. Heading out of Karakoseket, he slapped his thigh triumphantly. Happily, he strode down the road, envisioning the fortified dreams of his future.

34

THE WORD

THE THREE EXPLORERS CONTINUED their trek up Mt. Ararat. Zany remembered his parents before his conception: How Father Zany, in a fit of mento-physical eruption, gave the gift of his viscous and sticky Wow seed to mother Zany, how she carried this ovo- sperm dynamo nine months in her heating chamber before presenting his flesh-covered container to the world.

A fulfilling *possibility* occurred to Zany. Could this trip have already served its purpose? Could his search be *over?* True, Attila and Mashugi were still looking for the original Word. But was *he?* Did he really *need* such knowledge? Secretly, he realized he *already knew it!* What could the word be? No doubt, it concerned feelings of Wow! What else could it be? God knew the Word. Zany knew it, too. Probably, deep in their hearts, everyone knew it. Only few in the world dared to hear, follow its dictates, or admit they did. Why? Fear of public condemnation, scorn, and ridicule; they'd be called unsophisticated fools, naifs, dunces, or worse.

But Zany's years on the concert stage had habituated him to mixed audience reactions. Expressions of adulation, deni-

gration, or indifference were common occurrences for perform-
ers. Zany concerts had received reviews of every kind from
thousands of critics—so many, in fact, that he had long ago
stopped reading them. Besides, what did critics ever know
about his heart and musical purpose? True, they had to make
their living by writing reviews. But what did those reviews have
to do with *him?*

Zany ended his climb. He put down his knapsack and sat
down on a rock. Attila and Mashugi looked at him with questions in their eyes. "Go on without me," he said.

"Aha," said Mashugi.

"Yes," said Attila.

Etymologist and archeologist understood. They gave Zany
a long hug, said goodbye, and continuing their strenuous trek
up the mountain.

One year later, they returned. They had met a man named Noah
on top of Ararat. The white-haired sage had complained the
ark had fallen into terrible disrepair. By now, most of it had dis-
integrated. Its occupants had departed millennia before. Only
termites had remained to devour, bit by bit, its tasty cedars of
Lebanon.

Disappointed, Mashugi had merely said, "I thought termites
didn't eat cedar."

Noah had answered, "The ark was attacked by giant ante-
diluvian termites. Species were different then. If you want to
know more about these insects, read works by the ancient Ex-
egetikites, a little-known sect. Presently, they dwell near the
Black Sea. All are dedicated to the study of pre-biblical rodents,
insects, and mammalian life. Their leading scholars claim that
ancient termites were really mammals about the size of present-

day woodchucks; their teeth were as large as cucumbers and powerful enough to cut through steel, although, of course, that metal had not yet been invented."

Noah had given precise historical descriptions, not only of the ark's construction, but of the Flood itself. He had leaned on his oak cane as he explained. "After the great Maboul, ante-diluvian termites degenerated, diminished in size. Back then, the crunching power of their jaws was so great, many called them 'Ter Mights.' However, excessive munch pride angered the Lord. He turned them into ter mites. The Master did the same with Tyrannosaurus Rex. Once a proud, pugnacious king of the dinosaurs, hubris caused a reversal of his evolution. Dinosaurs devolved into salamanders. The termites diminished, became insects, still dangerous, but mere shadows of their ancient selves."

"My uncle Oscar in Tiberius is an exterminator," Mashugi had remarked.

Attila had then asked Noah if he knew about the Ur-sound, the Word itself. Where was it? Had he heard it? What did it sound like? The old man had looked at them before exclaiming, "What a question! WOW!"

Zany's intuitive knowledge had been confirmed.

The Word, a subtle, powerful, mystery, a cosmic vibration, exists everywhere. Once found, it is lost. Folks aware of its sound feel its power, dive into its energy, but never speak it. Pronouncing the Word materializes it and destroys its strength, subjecting it to limitations of space and time.

Zany descended Ararat. Reaching the foothills, stumbling less and less, he was soon walking with an easy gait. A smile of satisfaction and victory crossed his face. He began a slow jog, which turned into a run, then a sprint! Faster and faster sped his nimble legs gained as he jetted down the mountain path. His arms, light and nimble, now carried him past trees, streams, and verdant fields. A glorious shout of freedom burst from his lips!

"I have been out of tune for *years!*" he cried, smacking a tree with his hand and kicking a boulder. As it rolled down the mountain, he laughed with joy: "It's over, it's over! No more out of tune for me! I'm going home! Yes, yes!" Words streamed from his mouth, cleansing the nightmare year of dreary arm-chair sitting, lost daydreams, and dull, endless transitions. As Mama Zany had asked on the porch by the brook: "Can a sala-mander squawk with succulence?"

Now the Anatolian brook had roared back: "Indeed, it can!" Time to go home.

He cascaded down the hill. The Zany cry of freedom rico-cheted from the rocks, bounced among the flowers, echoed through the valley, and cascaded up the mountain, at last reach-ing the peaks of Ararat.

On his road up ahead, the sun beamed in Turkish. In the distance, he heard "WOW!" thundering from the peak of Mt. Ararat.

POSTHUMOUS TOURS

35

REBIRTH

WHEN ZOLTAN ZANY STOOD in the foothills of Mount Ararat, he felt the power of rebirth rush through his veins.

Limpid mountain air entered his hungry nostrils. Oxygen flowed through lungs and veins, igniting his freshly cleansed, naked soul. Fertile directions, accompanied by wild vistas and adventurous new paths of imagination, opened before him.

The violinist raised his arms to the heavens, and in Sufic cry of ecstasy, again shouted, "WOW!" The vibrations resounded through the valley. On the peak of Ararat, he spied a giant "W" rising. A zephyr blew an armchair-shaped cumulus cloud across the sky. Soon it disappeared behind a pine tree.

Silence: Zany listened. Sighing with satisfaction, he bowed to the sun, kissed the ground, and saluted the blue and boundless Turkish sky.

Facing the Western Anatolian plain, neck straight, athletic body erect, mind exploding, and spirit tuned and ready, he prepared for his future.

The adventurer now began two days of happy trekking. He danced over boulders, leapt from stream to stream, cracked ancient branches, and whistled erotically to the sprouting grass. Waving goodbye to Mt. Ararat, he inhaled deeply and savored the moment.

He reached a market in a small village. Broccoli, pickles, and asparagus spears lay spread on the Turkish vegetable stand to his right. "*Gun aydin,*" said Zany. He pointed to the broccoli. "Broccoli lunch, please."

The portly owner thanked him: "*Tessekur ederim.*" His imperial tone reminded Zany of Mehmet II, whose army had conquered Constantinople in 1453. The salesman added: "An emptied mind brings peace and wonder."

Next day, boarding the morning train to Ankara, Zany repeated the wise utterance of the vegetable mentor to himself. Hours later, passing the capital city, he asked himself: Who was he? Do I still *want* such a mentor? After fulfilling his voyage to Mt. Ararat, did he even need one? Perhaps at this stage of his life, simple de-mentia was best. Riding on wings of celestial madness was a path worthy of his future!

Nevertheless, Zany felt grateful for the philosophic advice. He headed towards Istanbul armed with desire to learn and the virtue of a brain filled with emptiness.

Ararat had done its job. A new violin vision stood in order. No more reason to visit mountain tops. At last he felt capable, not only of bringing a high-altitude attitude back to the USA, but of offering it to future audiences.

The train passed Urgup. Dr. Zany considered his past. *I've gone past the limits of violin technique. I need to embrace something rarer.*

36

ZANY ENTERPRISES

A T THE TIME ZOLTAN Zany attended college at University of Rochester in upstate New York, he'd taken courses in anatomy and dissection. He had even considered becoming a medical doctor. The future concert artist enjoyed talking to cadavers and skeletons about the afterlife.

Although the dissected bodies and their various parts had never been notably responsive, Zany thought he'd heard whispers, mumbles, mutters—even an occasional word about "The Place."

Excited by the possibility of such a location, he had spoken with St. James and other business-savvy colleagues about its future travel potential. They'd suggested meeting Warren Bagdanovitchavitch, a Serbian soothsayer turned entrepreneur. Then eighty-eight years old, the former Belgrade police chief had studied tourism under the tutelage of Joseph Stalin in Russia during the early fifties. After the Georgian dictator's death, he had taken Yugo World Tours to America, and, after receiving an illegal tourism license from the New York State Licensing and Sewage Board, set up his One World Travel agency at the Fifty-seventh Street subway station in Manhattan. Presently, he owned fourteen agencies, each located in a major American city. From his concert tour along the Drina River, Zany knew Serbian business practices had certain "twists" and "unique approaches" that might sharpen his own travel skills and business acumen.

Warren B's One World Travel was the only American company offering complimentary calendars to both Russian magnates and western diplomats.

Zany met the company president in his spacious New York office. The Serbian entrepreneur was sitting behind an enormous mahogany desk beside a window overlooking the East River.

"Welcome," he said in a deep gravelly voice. "So you are interested in travel?" He tugged on his suspenders as he brushed a few ashes from his sleeveless brown shirt.

"I am."

"Perhaps you'd like to start a travel company?" Mr. B let the idea sink in, then added, "Perhaps you'd like to buy this one?"

Reaching into his drawer, he pulled out a pistol. Seeing it in his hand and realizing his mistake, he quickly returned it, and in its place drew out a Cuban cigar, which he offered to Zany as he said, "Fear is a wonderful thing."

"I like philosophy, Mr. B. I'll keep that tip in mind."

"I have many good ideas, Mr. Zany, but fear is my best one. It increases your focus. 'The fearful traveler is the happy traveler.' Learn to use fear, Mr. Zany, and you'll be a happy traveler, too."

Zany knew about fear. He also liked the idea of starting a travel company. A fresh breath of confidence blew through his brain. "I've swayed minds and hearts performing for thousands," he said. "But now I need something new. And I'd like it to have a royal touch. I've always liked kings. If I started my own travel business, I'd be king of my company. By combining attributes of Moses, Pepin the Short, Charles V, Julius Caesar, Gandhi, and Winston Churchill, I could lead my travelers to new realms—and in the process, unchain and uplift my formerly tortured soul."

He left the Bagdanovitchavitch meeting riding a current of enthusiasm. First, he called friends, family, and neighbors, attempting to gather brains and brawn for his travel project. After a week of phone calls, he was finally able to organize a few worthies to meet and discuss his travel company.

At 9:00 a.m. the next Monday morning, July 24, Zany gathered his new "business partners" in his living room. "Blood flow to the buttocks stimulates brain power as it increases circulation," he said to himself as he arranged hard, straight-backed, wooden chairs in a semi-circle. He opened the curtains wide. Blue sky appeared, and rays of shining sun flooded his living room office with light. The neophyte entrepreneur finished off preparations by adding a special scent, created and bottled by Barnes Business Aromas of Little Rock, Arkansas, released an aroma of bacon, Sardinian sardines, fried clams, and garlic sauce from the kitchen.

At ten o'clock the doorbell rang out "William Tell Overture," by Rossini, followed by the Prelude to Wagner's *Parsifal*. One by one, partners of the new enterprise filed in, sat down in the semi-circle facing Zany, and waited in silence and entrepreneurial anticipation.

Who were these insightful, creative paragons of the future?

Facing a gold framed oil portrait of Helmoltz von Poppowick, author of the businessman's bible, *Heilbeitung von Recht Fuss*, these adventurous servants sat in the following order:

1. *Tall, elegant former successful businessman and basketball player, the stately St. James.*
2. *Narrow, squat, ugly, the bearded Mongolian molecule, Ghengis Kohan.*
3. *Lean and narrow, AK-47 in hand, Attila Zany.*
4. *Round and chubby, wearing an green apron, bearing a set of kitchen utensils, the ever-wise and practical Martha.*
5. *Invisible but still present, a silent partner sitting in distant Colorado, representing the furthest branch of Zany Enterprises, Brunhilde Zany.*

St. James was the first to speak. Adjusting his tie and turning to face the others, he said, "We must think outside the box."

"I agree," Attila added. "Outside the box is good. Further outside is better. Beyond the box is best! Car, bus, train, plane, rocket, space ship. Think beyond the material plane."

"There you go with your whacked-off notions," said Ghengis, kneeling before a miniature medieval Mongolian horse cart, a business talisman created by his personal shaman, the Siberian wizard Boris Tachmanovitch.

"Stop complaining about my son!" Brunhilde insisted in a firm, disembodied voice from Colorado. "I brought him up on salads."

"Leave family squabbles out of this!" Zany snarled at the apparition. "Come on, everyone. Let's move the conversation along. In order to make our mark, we need *real* ideas. We've already named our company Zany Enterprises. Let's drive our stake into the future by starting with a zany idea: Let dreams and reality merge at our doorstep!"

"I like it," Attila agreed.

"Dream-reality combos are often big sellers in the market-place," St. James observed.

Ghengis nodded. "Yes! It's the Mongolian way. Combine practical with visionary. Ghengis Khan would be proud."

"I prefer goulash," said Martha.

Zany jumped to his feet. "Right! Thank you, my business partners. Together we've found our direction: Both visionary and practical."

Attila, remembering his economics course in Bustard U. "Where is the void in the travel marketplace?" he asked. "We'll compete by offering something *new,* tours to rarely visited places. Or better, organize tours to destinations *never* visited! We could dominate that market!"

"Attila, my Hungarian offspring and lover of domination, I'm proud of you." Zany patted his chest. "Finally, all the college money we laid out for you is paying off."

Martha stepped in with a touch of Teutonic doubt. "What destinations are unique? What tours have never been done before?" She rose from her wicker chair, ambled into the kitchen, stirred a pot of waiting stew, and, called out from beside the stove, "A vegetable tour of the Ukraine, perhaps."

"I don't see many tours to Mongolia," Ghengis offered. "We *could* do the Gobi Desert. To my knowledge, water hole tours from Western Europe are totally unknown. We'll call it: 'Great Gobi Water Holes.'"

"Didn't Marco Polo travel through Mongolia?" St. James asked. "I believe he visited the Gobi. That trip has been done before."

Attila recalled his college History of Dismembered Empires course, with its special emphasis on Venetian adventurers. "Apostle, Marco did it so long ago that, today, no one remembers. We could refresh the destination, throw in extra horse carts, motorcycles, air-conditioned bus, add high-end accommodations, and reach a market of modern travelers."

"I don't do 'modern,'" snarled Ghengis. "I do *manly*. 'Modern' is for sissies."

"How about a relatively unknown country," asked Zany. "A tour of Hungary featuring Magyar Musical Madness. I'd like to visit the land of my roots."

"That's nice for you," St. James said, "but it's not a business plan. Hungary is a relatively known destination. So are most eastern European countries. We must strive for uniqueness, offer a difference, find new customers, even create a new market."

The others agreed. Martha brought in tea from the kitchen and served it to the team of consultants now sitting in silence, pondering the problem.

Finally, Attila spoke up. "How about Mars?" he asked. "No one's been *there*."

"Planets are good," Zany agreed. "Also the moon."

Martha rested a soft, stabilizing hand on Zany's shoulder. "Interplanetary travel may be too advanced for our enterprises at the moment. Better something more practical, a destination we can attack immediately, tomorrow."

Attila heard Brunhilde's virtual voice pop out from her Colorado mountain cabin: "Travel outside the box, beyond the ordinary. Adventures are dreams in disguise. Consider the absurd. New visions are often frightening. Never-been-done- before has its glory. . . ."

Attila mumbled into his shirt. "How about reincarnation?"

Suddenly, a light sprang from Zany's eyes. Sparks fell as he opened them wide. Raising his right hand, he pointed his index finger to the sky, and shouted triumphantly, "*Thank* you, Attila.

I've got it! Let's do the *hereafter!* Hereafter Travel! We'll grab the future *and* present all at once."

Martha forced a cup of tea into Zany's trembling hand. But his excitement was too great, and he dropped it on the floor. As the spearmint-flavored liquid spread across the rug, Zany, oblivious to the damage, went on. "All people die. What happens then? Where do they go? How do they spend their time? What is there to *do* in the hereafter? Up to now, there has been an absence of options. Many of our current intellectuals think they go *nowhere.* But we at Zany Enterprises know better. We *know* where they go, or at least, where they *can* go. To the Great Beyond! And *we* can make their *travel arrangements.* It's a wide-open market. We'll dominate it!"

Zany's business partners froze in place, stunned. Attila blinked. St. James tapped his foot, and a twitch appeared in his jaw. Kohan scratched his belly until his shirt ripped.

"I'll get more tea," Martha finally said. She rose and left the room. Minutes later she brought it in and served it in dainty cups. Not a thank-you arose from a soul. All sat and drank in the silence.

An hour later, Attila sighed and shot a round from his AK-47 into the floor. This woke up the room. Ghengis stopped fidgeting with his shirt; St. James blinked. Even Brunhilde, in her distant Colorado haunt, seemed alerted.

St. James cleared his throat. "Give Zoltan credit for thinking out of the box. But can his idea be taken seriously? It is so outlandish and crazy. . .it just might work!"

"I don't like the name," said Attila. "'Hereafter' has no ring, zing, or etymological significance. Better would be: Posthumous."

"Ah, what a boy!" shouted Zany. "I like it!" He slapped

his thigh in happiness; he ran around the room to slap every-one's thigh. *"Posthumous Tours* it is!"

Zany's enthusiasm, shouts, and thigh slapping sparked new interest in the company.

Ghengis looked skeptical, but slowly his question mark face contorted into an explanation point. "It could work."

Martha turned to St. James. "Apostle, you're the only one here with any business experience. We respect your opinion. You didn't become a millionaire gardener out of thin air. If *you* claim Dr. Zany's mad tour idea is worthy, perhaps it is."

Attila cleaned his gun. "I like new adventures."

Brunhilde smiled.

"We should explore this further," Ghengis said.

Pleased, Zany looked around the room. "I'm glad my business partners are open to new ideas."

Attila shot a few rounds into the floor. "Exploring the unknown is an adventure."

"We all need adventures," Ghengis agreed.

"But how will we do it?"

St. James stepped in. "First, we need a business plan. During the years developing and leading my company, I worked with many kinds of entrepreneurs—funeral parlor directors, cremation specialists, and obituary writers are the first that come to mind."

St. James fell silent as he dredged his memory for his old business friends. He reached into his pocket and pulled out an address book filled with venture capitalists, bankers, financial analysts, entrepreneurs, and marketing people. The others waited, hopefully.

He took a sip of tea. "The most out-of-the-box thinker I know is a former funeral-parlor owner. His name is Aristotle "Santorini" Athanatopoulis—'Arty' to his friends. His company, Aegean Cremations, or 'No Body Cremations,' once hit fifty on the stock market. Presently, its valuation is of over sixty million dollars! He's also a prominent apiarist and keeps a dozen hives of active bees in his oven. Clients often call him 'Honey.' Born on Santorini, Arty claims his ancestors belonged to the Kingdom of Atlantis, but that most disappeared when the volcano erupted and destroyed the island. Let's hire him as a consultant. Shall I call him?"

37

ZANY TRAVEL

"YES!" ZANY'S TONGUE WAS rolling hot. "Our Zany Enterprises will spread its travel gospel throughout this world and the next! Anoint future buyers. Drive buses filled with clients to ancient archaeological sites! Employ animals, vegetables, blend organic and inorganic, mix compounds. None will be excluded in our vast and glorious venture! Tin, gold dust, copper, plus inorganic chemical friends, oat pellets, grains, soy beans, corn. In fact, all commodities."

"Your crazy mind is on *fire!*" Genghis shouted. "Where's the extinguisher?" He was about to run into the hallway when Attila jumped up, squeezed his father's cheek, slapped his face, and said, "Hold on, Pop. Wait a minute. Slow down. Explain yourself. What do you mean by a *travel* agency? You know you *hate* travel."

Zany calmed himself. "That's true, my son. Years of concertizing have weakened, even squelched, my travel desires. In fact, they have long ago departed, along with my desire to give concerts. That's why I'm making *you* president of our company."

"Me?" Attila shook his head. A vague feeling of panic pummeled his stomach. "I don't *know* anything about *travel*."

"That's why you're the best candidate!"

"But I don't *want* to be president. I don't even want a *job*."

Zany looked directly into the eyes of his confused, frightened, and unhappy son. "Attila, this idea has been cooking in my brain a long time. You're lost, alone, and your life is a fumble. Although you graduated from Bustard U, what use is a degree in *linguistics?* As Mama Zany told me at the police station after I started my first forest fire at the age of nine, 'A specific direction and personal goal straightens the bent brain.' My son, what you need is meaningful path, a higher purpose shining above you. As president of our company, you will have exactly that."

Attila pondered this. Instinctively, he squeezed his AK-47 trigger finger, but so softly no bullets came out. He stared at the floor, the ceiling and around the room; he waited, hoping the eyes riveted upon him in anticipation would give an answer.

After ten minutes of silence, he finally said, "Well, I don't *mind* being lost. In fact, I like it."

His father countered with a genetic survey: "Enjoyment of the lost state is a family tradition," he said, resting a sympathetic hand on Attila's shoulder. "Another tradition is: Experimental floundering must not go on too long. If this happens, you will degenerate, and soon enter states of lethargy, depression, and self-destruction. Your mother and I never wanted that fate for you. Besides, it's fun to be a president. It creates growth spurts, impresses women, and may even help you find a wife."

"I'm not ready for marriage."

"Someday you will be."

"Never! Tied down? Are you kidding? As our Bustard entomologist/etymologist hermit professor, Patrick Harry, author of the best selling *Fireflies: Beacons of Freedom*, proclaimed in class: 'Give me liberty or give me death!'"

Zany sighed in frustration. "*Henry*, Patrick *Henry*. No wonder your mother became a chemist." Then, nodding with paternal understanding, he went on. "Nevertheless, I *know* what's best for you. Until your molecules are correctly arranged and your mind is straightened out, a presidency is the safest and healthiest place for you."

Attila considered his options. Since his trip to Mt. Ararat ended, he'd had no place to go. Even his fevered linguistic studies had halted. He was at a standstill. "I don't know," he speculated. "I've still got so much growing up to do before I burden myself with such big responsibilities. I want to live a bit more before I go into business."

The wise, experienced St. James stepped in: "Life does not *end* when you go into business," he explained. "In fact, I'd say that's when *life begins!* Nothing expands your mind like business."

"Yes," his father agreed. "Plus, through the travel business you'll *see the world!* Think of *countries* you'll visit! Imagine shooting an AK-47 in Tunisia, Thailand, France, Brazil, India, the Antarctic! . . . What could be better?"

"Really. . . ?"

"I like the company name, too," St. James added. "It has the ring of truth."

"Travel with travail," Martha called from the kitchen.

Genghis Kohan's skepticism had disappeared. An unexpected enthusiasm bubbled up. "With the Posthumous Tours brand name, you'll travel with pride," he pointed out. "Use your brain for direction, your legs as adventure spokes. In Mongolia, it is common knowledge that the rectus femoris was Marco Polo's favorite muscle."

38

TRANSFORMATION

AN ENTHUSIASTIC, TRANSFORMED ATTILA descended from his attic room. He found his father sitting in his armchair, reading the entertainment section of the *New York Times*. The Con Edison repair man had just left, and the living room still smelled of gas from the oven leak. Attila nodded a quick hello to Martha, who was cleaning the kitchen stove with a Brillo pad.

The lad turned to his father. "Pop, I've got good news!"

Zany lifted his reading glasses. "Friedrich Popvanohausen, the Serbo-Bavarian fiddler, is performing his orchestral version of Beethoven's 'Kreutzer Sonata.' It's with the Berlin Philharmonic next Friday. I'm going. "

"Father, I know you'll want to hear this."

"Come with me."

"Pop—"

"You'll *like* this concert. I spoke to the stage manager, Big John O'Brogan. He confirmed that weapons were allowed in the hall. You can even sit in our box seats with your AK-47."

"Pop, I'm—"

"So you'll go?" Zany's eyes focused on his son's trembling, excitement-pumped lips. "Aha—huh, Attila my boy. . . what did you say?"

"I'm accepting the presidency position."

"Really?" Zany put aside his newspaper. "What made you decide that?"

"It came to me in a ray of sunlight."

"Quite a development. Are you sure it's for you?"

"Absolutely."

"How will you go about this?"

"Father, I've learned the 'how' from you. I'm taking it a step further. I'll follow the etymological road, shooting my AK- 47 in the places I prefer. I'll become my own leader. However, since the business world has customers who often disagree with me, I've decided to lead them as well."

"That's quite grandiose. There are lots of customers in the world. How do you expect to show them a path?"

"I won't be able to lead everybody. But I don't have to. Just a few will do. My own group, my own tribe. . . *our* own group, *our* own tribe."

"Attila, how did you get any of these notions from me? I'm not a tribal leader, or follower. I'm an artist, an individualist. I don't *belong*."

"Ah, but you do, father. You may not wear a feather, have a totem pole, or worship with a shaman, but you belong to something. You are. . . or were. . . a solo violinist. You belong to the clan of musicians, the music tribe."

"I suppose you could put it that way."

Attila rubbed his hands together. "Father, here's my plan. As president of our tour company, my first question is: Where do we start? The answer, of course, is Hungary. Place of origin, home of your ancestors. There are also great musicians there, especially violinists. We'll court, gather, and mine those musicians. Our company will have a special niche. We'll offer special itineraries for music and travel lovers."

". . .Interesting."

"Then we'll set up meetings with Hungarian musicians you know. Our symphonic or soloist lovers can talk to them, hear them play in small, intimate settings, touch their coat sleeves, get their autographs. Our customers will have a personal contact with greatness that no other company can offer! We'll promote, sell, and bring our tours to lovers of music all over the world. We'll dominate the market!"

Zany sat up straight. "This unique approach is worthy of my son," he said proudly. Hunching and straightening in his armchair, he considered the idea further. His initial enthusiasm met an inner resistance: "But I don't want to contact these so-called 'artists.' They pervert their performances, miss notes, savage the conductors—"

"Pop, that's all besides the point. We don't really care how they play. It's a *tour* company, not a musical organization. We want to meet them, understand them as Hungarian people who happen to also be first-rate musicians. And if they happen to be second- or third-rate, that's okay, too. Plus, all of them speak Hungarian; they're an etymologist's dream."

"I don't—"

"Imagine it, Pop. Customers will not only see historic sites, but will *become* the sites! Locals will flock to see us, just as we flock to see them. History, diplomacy, even religion all tied into one. Just as Hungarians affect and influence us, our program and itinerary will affect and influence them!

"Pop, one thing you do know well is music; you also know the best musicians in the world. You can arrange home meetings. We can also greet them at the Festival, mingle with their fans, become part of their scene. This is the age of social media! We'll learn about Hungary through its people, mainly its musicians. We'll invent a never-done-before visiting style. We'll create a *new way to travel!*"

BUSINESS

THE ZANY GROUP MET, to plan business strategy, every Monday morning in the Xenophon Diner.

Overlooking a parking lot at a bend in the scenic Hackensack River, the Xenophon had an attractive mix of quiet breakfast diners and tasty Greek morsels to "keep the crowd coming."

When Thanatos Ianni Protokarapoulos entered, St. James waved to him. "Hey, Teddy," he called, "Come join us."

The stocky restaurant owner strode over, extended his hand first to St. James, and offered it in chiropathic friendship to Attila. "Happy to see you."

Attila viewed the hairy hand with its twisted index finger. Elbowing his mentor, he said, "I don't want to meet anybody. I need to get away, think things over." Teddy watched as the lad jumped up from his seat and raced to a distant corner table.

"Give him time," St. James suggested by way of apology. "He still has doubts about the big decisions he has to make. Matter of commitment. How's business?"

The two friends discussed vicissitudes of the restaurant. A dark-haired waitress wearing a T-shirt from the Brinkenhoffen

Wine Cellars of Bavaria raced from table to table, served plates of souvlaki and cups of coffee. Stopping at Attila's table, her eyebrows rose. "Yes?"

"I'll take a glass of wine mixed with retsina," he ordered. The waitress looked at him quizzically but disappeared into the kitchen.

She returned, placed a full glass before him, and moved on. Attila took a sip, relaxed, leaned back, gazed out the window, and visited the confused studio of his mind. As the waitress bent to pluck an empty salad plate from the adjacent table, he leaned towards her. "What should I do with my life?"

"Order french toast." She turned to take an order of bacon and scrambled eggs from a heavy-set woman with dark glasses, wearing a Greek sailor's cap. Writing it down on her scratch pad, she glanced again at Attila. Doubts and questions clouded the lad's mind. "Did I make the right decision? Should I accept the presidency?" He took another sip of wine. "My father is smart. Sure, he's off the wall, but he's not wall*paper*. His advisors offer excellent counseling. St. James is no dope, the Mongolian Molecule has lots of worldly experience, Martha is in the game, too, and so is my favorite Persian seer, Zoroaster. True, he hasn't entered the picture yet, but who cares? I like the way he disguises his Greek origin behind that Persian name! Very *myster*-ious, a true Greek root of the word. I prefer hidden meanings. Names are significant."

He drained his glass. Peeking from behind a cloud, the morning sun threw a beam across his table. Things were looking up. He felt better. A shiver of control passed through his softly clenched fist. Slowly, the fingers hardened. His presidential decision was reaffirmed. Suddenly, Attila raised his fork high in the air. The pointed utensil descended in a flash, stabbing the picture of Athen's Acropolis on his place mat setting. The table trembled as he cried, "Yes! Mama was right. I *need* to be president! Such a position will put bones in my blood, fire in my stool, iron in my heart. Leadership fills one with purpose. Assuming responsibility for an agency will forge a powerful direction in my life!"

A happy smile emerged and spread over Attila's face. Placing a seven-dollar tip beside his plate, he rose, thanked the folks at the adjacent table, and moved to the Zany Group Travel conference. Purpose, direction, and adventure lay ahead.

"Good morning, everyone!" A renewed Attila eased himself next to St. James, a quirky grin of secret intention on his face. Nodding hello to Teddy, he looked directly at his business mentor. "When do we start?" he asked.

"Start what?" St. James asked.

Teddy leaned over. "Yes, what?"

Attila shot a thumb in Teddy's direction. "Who's he?"

"That's Teddy. He owns this restaurant. Start what?"

Attila extended a friendly hand to Teddy. "Glad to meet you. I like your french toast. Good wine and restina, too."

"*Poli kala. Ef charisto,* my friend."

"An excellent and unusual breakfast," St. James added. A long pause ensued. "Well. . . ?"

Attila spoke in an assured voice. "I'm ready."

"Ready for what?"

"Responsibility and adventure. Ready to assume the presidency of Zany Enterprises! I even have a company motto. *Onward, upward, and sideward!*"

"*That* was a quick transformation," said St. James, surprised and pleased.

"I'd call it a resurrection," Teddy added.

St. James turned to the Corinthian. "Why do you always add a religious element? You don't even know this kid."

"I know the Lord," Teddy answered. "Kids come in all sizes. They're just extensions of Him."

"I've never agreed with your view of children. When are you going to join the secular saviors of the twenty-first century?"

Teddy's face reddened. He slammed his open palm on the table. "You call those communists saviors?" he shouted.

"Let's not start this again," St. James said, grabbing the restaurant owner by the sleeve and pulling him back to his seat.

The waitress glared at her boss. "Knock it off, Teddy,"

"Hey, what about me?" Attila growled. "I'm the one you're supposed to be talking about."

"Who cares about you?" said Teddy. "The pawn is a mere thorn when the King's power is on display. Your thoughts are nothing."

St. James sighed. "Drop the religious stuff for now. The lad has just made a positive statement filled with high confidence, context, and meaning. In fact, the Lord would be proud."

Teddy calmed down,. He looked at the recessed lighting in the ceiling and further upward for guidance. "You're right about that."

St. James raised his hand to a passing waiter. "Three coffees, please."

"I hate coffee," said Attila.

"I'm not a drinker either," Teddy added.

The apostle broke in, "These coffees aren't for you. They're for me. Coffee improves my vision. A major transformation is taking place before our eyes. Let's explore it further." He placed his hand gently on Attila's trigger finger. "What's going on?"

Attila wet his lips; his forehead wrinkled as it perspired. Conflicts among instinct, emotion, intellect, etymological purpose, athletic dynamism, worldly desires, and celestial radiance were raging in his mind. "I was sitting in the corner," he explained, "when the sun. . .a light. . .burst across the table. Suddenly, all my parts came together. I knew *what* to do, *where* to go, and how to *do* it. Scattered meanings fused into a giant sphere with the plosive grand capital *P* of PURPOSE written across it. Linguists know about the letter P. They know from ancient history that, when first written by the Phoenicians, reconstituted by Anglo-Saxon mystics, pressed by Danish seafarers and Greenland explorers, onionized by Snurri Snurelson's Icelandic sagas, pisticulated by Middle-English-speaking Zanzibar monkeys, melted into its iconic poster-shape by Byzantine monks, before its garlic-sprinkled finalization by post-Renaissance deacons that the letter *P* meant Progress beyond the posterior; the grand Push forward. It blended plosive and fricative into clear paths of *my* future."

St. James raised his hand to halt the monologue. "That's all very interesting, Attila. What does it mean?"

"The meaning is clear. *P* also stands for President. I'm accepting my father's offer."

St. James's eyes gleamed. "Wonderful! Your father will be happy."

Ghengis leaned forward. "I am, too."

Martha nodded in smiling contentment.

Teddy rose to shake the lad's hand. "Such decisions are life changing. Congratulations."

PLANNING AND STRATEGY

The following Monday, all seven consultants of the Zany Group met again in the Xenophon Diner to plan strategy.

Zoltan Zany, Martha, Attila, Gengis, St. James, Brunhilde Ever-in-Absentia Zany, and Teddy, their newest member, sat around their business table in a corner by the window. Outside, under a cloudless sky, they saw the waters of Hackensack River pleasantly flowing. A man fishing from a canoe, and two kayaks on their way to the Atlantic, floated by. After ordering plates of souvlaki, spanakopita, hamburgers, and celebration wine, they ate, uttering pleasantries. While easing digestion with sips of coffee, Teddy rose, pushed back his salt-and-pepper mop of hair, and said: "Friends, welcome to my restaurant. I am happy to be invited by such esteemed intellectuals. Holding your weekly business meetings here in the Xenophon brings me honor and profit. A wise decision, indeed. There is no better place in which to discuss the future of your enterprise. Here, business plans are born, grow, and develop while strategy, itself an ancient Greek word for 'general,' thrives."

He placed a hand on St. James's shoulder. "I know business.

My friend here will vouch for that." He locked eyes with St. James for an extended moment and scanned the table for grease spots and gravy stains.

"Let me tell you a little known fact about the Xenophon. Eight years ago, the spot on which we now sit was a garbage dump. They called it 'land-fill' at the time. St. James and I stood here, knee-deep in refuse, covered by flies, with handkerchiefs over our noses to shield us from the stink; only our boots protecting us from rats scurrying underfoot. Nevertheless, even as we stood rooted in filth, St. James's optimism and positive viewpoint carried the day. 'Teddy, this is a perfect spot for a dining establishment!' he said. 'Buy the land! Upon this dump, a restaurant shall rise!'

"'Outlandish!' I protested. 'I can't do it. Such an idea is totally foreign to me!'

"'Precisely,' he answered. 'That's why you should do it! And name it Xenophon Diner! As you know, Xenophon means "foreign."'

"Such a wonderful Greek word. And my own diner named after it! In that moment, I jumped from depths of absurdity and negativity to heights of hope and entrepreneurship! Apocalypse, yes! First comes idea, then action. On that day, Xenophon Diner was born!"

Teddy raised his wine glass. "Thomas St. James, I want to thank you for your service to me!"

Everyone at the table applauded.

Ghengis elbowed the Apostle. "I didn't know your first name was Thomas."

"I didn't even know you *had* a first name," said Zany.

St. James chuckled softly, pushed back his chair, and lifted his wine glass. "Here's to my Irish mother, Mary O'Grady, a

Cork of a lady." Raised his glass even higher, he went on: "Here's to my gallant Galician Spanish father Juan Sevirante Postales from Santiago de Compostela.

"He was the first to tell me that the city of Santiago was named after me. Or was it vice versa?" St. James smiled at his humor. "In any case, that's how I got my name.

"Although some of you have spoken with me for years, none of you really *know* me. Time to change all that. We're starting out on a new venture. In order to succeed, we'll have to know and trust each other. A tall order for such a scattered, individualistic, brainy, artistic group.

"So, to begin the LRP—learning and revelation process— I'll tell you about myself."

A long silence ensued. Attila ordered some french toast and another glass of wine from the waitress. The sun, rising another inch in the morning sky, threw a brief shadow across the north side of the breakfast table. Finally, Martha murmured, "Well. . . ?"

At last, St. James spoke. "Reticence is the key to knowledge," he explained cryptically.

"What's that supposed to mean?" Ghengis asked.

"I really don't know," the saint admitted. "That's what my father always said to my mother before he took out the garbage. It could mean anything. But *I* interpret it this way: The world and its inhabitants are mysteries. One never knows the future, or even the past. Life is the fiction you make up as you go along. Daily you write a new script. I've found this philosophy to be true in my business and personal dealings. I believe it will be very effective as we grow and develop our tour group."

"You could be right," said Teddy. "After five years in the

restaurant business, how it works is still a mystery to me."

"Right. Teddy, you and I are the only ones here with any business experience. Our knowledge and risk-taking abilities will be powerful tools in this new venture. How to build an itinerary? What destinations shall we explore? What about insurance, guides, and luggage? What airlines, trains, or buses will fit our travel plans? Most important, how do we find customers?"

"All good questions," Teddy concurred.

"What about you, apostle?" Attila prodded. "Why believe *you*? Why should we trust your judgment?"

St. James rubbed his chin, slowly nudged his thoughts from mouth to brain, and began a short historical account: "After my birth in Cork, Mother looked down at me and cried, 'Not the best beginning!' One year later, our family emigrated to the USA. She never forgot the town of her origin. She longed for its salty streets and daily reminded my father about what she considered his faulty decision to move the family across the ocean. 'I miss Ireland. I miss sunny Cork,' she reminded my brother and me as she served us breakfast every morning. 'If not for Cork, Ireland would sink.'"

"A negative beginning," Teddy concluded.

St. James sipped his coffee. Martha winced at the popping sound of his audible gulp. The morning sun, dimmed by a cumulus cloud, inched higher in the sky. Shadows crossed the table.

"Indeed," St. James agreed, "I've been fighting negativity all my life."

"Not a problem," said Teddy. "Negative, positive, it really doesn't matter that much, since All is One."

"Don't give me that Buddhist-Pythagorean crap," the Apostle snarled. "I'm sick of it. When will you give up this silly idealism? Learn to run a restaurant in typical Western materialistic fashion."

Teddy's soothing voice calmed the room. "My good friend, the dining business is an illusion. My restaurant is an illusion. Material reality is an illusion. All is One."

"What's the use," sighed the saint in frustration. "We'll never agree about any of this."

"The *travel* business will bring us together," said Teddy. The The confident tone in his definitive statement surprised the Apostle.

"Oh? How is that?"

"Travel is universal. Everyone travels."

"Oh, yeah. Well, maybe you're right. "St James considered further. "In fact, you *are* right. Let's talk destination and itinerary. Where is the Zany group going? Where shall we start?"

"I say Hungary!" Dr. Zany declared.

"Hungary is a joke," Ghengis insisted. "*Mongolia* is the only true destination."

Attila looked wistfully at his father. "How about Colorado? We could visit Ma."

Martha shook her head. "Colorado, Mongolia, Hungary, are entres, mere *vorspeise*. *Germany* is the only country worth visiting."

"I don't mind Germany," said the doctor. "As long as we visit Hungary first. Then we can perhaps add the land of Beethoven, Bach, Mozart, Brahms, and Bubenhoffer von Pleistocene as an extension."

"Who's Pleistocene?" asked Attila.

"A little-known, ancient violinist from Dusseldorf. Some say he is already dead. Others, that he never lived."

"Living or dead is besides the point," cried Teddy. "Zoltan, you're made a perfect entry into one of my long-time tour ideas: Let's create an *underground* tour. I mean, *really* underground. Let's visit Hades! We'll check out Greek mythology. Besides, since the underground housing market collapsed, prices down there are pretty low. Hotels and ground services would be cheap."

"Totally impractical," hissed St. James. "Another one of your hair-brained ideas."

"Wait a minute." Zany had raised a finger. "I think Teddy's idea may have some merit. Long ago, in college, as a one-month pre-med student, while I studied cadavers, I conceived the idea of *Posthumous Tours,* a service dedicated to procrastinators, tardy travelers, those who 'registered too late.' Teddy's Hades travel idea might be right for us."

"It certainly fits reincarnation philosophy," said Attila. "All Buddhists and Pythagoreans believe in reincarnation."

"So do restaurant owners," Teddy added.

"So do I," said Zany.

"I like cars, too," Genghis threw in.

St. James sighed. "This is all beside the point. Alive or dead, it depends on what kind of customers we want? And, of course, what kind of travelers will want us? Why should they choose *our* company?"

"Because we're the best!" Attila declared.

"We don't even *exist* yet," Martha uttered in practical tone.

"Oh, I'm sure eventually we'll be good," said St. James. "Nevertheless, as a company, as a business, we have to realize that not everyone will want our product service. And just as customers will want certain things from us, *we* will want certain things from our customers, namely, a Zany traveling attitude."

"What's *that?*" Attila asked.

"An attitude that goes beyond positive or negative, right or wrong. We need to find our fan club, travelers of a certain mind-set, one filled with a spirit of adventure, humor, wonder, and patience."

Zany agreed. "Sounds like a good start."

"Isn't that a lot to ask from a customer?" Genghis asked. "Attila the Hun, my ancestor, never asked that of warriors, nor did Temujin, nor the great Ghengis Khan himself of their Mongolian hordes. When they sacked Central Asia, southern Russia, and Europe, no one said anything about wonder. Certainly not humor or patience. Pillage and rapine, that was the way to go! Add a good horse, steady bow, and slab of riding meat, and soon you've got an empire!"

"We're not that kind of company," said St. James

Attila pondered the Mongolian questions. "But we *could* use a horde of customers. We'd make lots of money."

"Money is good," St. James agreed. "And obviously, you need it to run a company. But in the long run, quality is more important."

"Ghengis Khan ran a quality tour," the Mongolian molecule pointed out.

"Oh, Ghengis," snarled Martha. "Get serious. This is the modern world, not the thirteenth century."

"What do you know, woman?" the molecule shouted back. "You're just a cook."

"With thirteen Ph. D.'s," Zany reminded him.

"An *educated* idiot, then!"

A smiling waitress came over. Her black hair fell over one eye as she asked: "More coffee, anyone?"

"We're busy," snapped Genghis. "Go away!" Her smile quickly faded, then vanished as she went to the next table.

"At least I'm German," Martha commented with icy calm.

"Stop fighting!" Attila shouted. "We're here to organize a business. Let's move on."

LEADERSHIP, PRESIDENCY, AND BUSINESS

A WEEK LATER, ST. JAMES was sitting alone with Attila at a corner table in the Xenophon during lunch break. Their waiter, a short, squat, swarthy fellow wearing a sports jacket over his Xenophon Diner T-shirt, brought two menus to the table. St. James read through them while Attila examined the spelling of *moussaka* and *spanakopita*. Polishing up his best Epirotic Greek, and adding the thick Dorian accent he'd picked up from his college roommate, Lefteris "Lefty" Karazagorisokakis, a Sarakatsan from Iannina who had taught him how to weave a Pindus Mountain shepherd's hut, Attila smiled to the waiter, and said, *"Thelo ena moussaka."*

The waiter nodded, returned to the kitchen, and soon returned carrying a plate of souvlaki and a burger. Placing the Greek dish in front of St. James, he handed Attila a hamburger.

"This is not what I asked for," Attila protested.

Squinting quizzically, the waiter cocked his head. *"Que?"*

"Moussaka!" Attila repeated.

"Ah, *entiendo*." The waiter scurried off and soon came back with the house special, a mega-deluxe jumbo cheeseburger smothered in bacon bits, lettuce, tomato, onions, and peppers. He lowered the plate on the table before Attila with a soft tap. "*De nada.*" The Guatemalan turned to customers at the adjacent table.

St. James bit into his souvlaki, chewed slowly, savored the tasty lamb, and swallowed with satisfaction. Then he leaned towards Dr. Zany's son. "A company president holds the future of the enterprise within his visionary mind," he explained. "The Florentine Renaissance man, diplomat, political philosopher, and musician Nicolo Machiavelli wrote, in *De Principatibus,* published five years after his death in 1532, that *a leader has to be both loved and feared.* Attila, your father, my long-time friend and colleague, has chosen you to lead our fledgling travel company. But in order to fulfill his vision, you must *want* and *need.*" He paused, considered, took another bite of souvlaki, and reconsidered. "Actually, even want and need are not enough. Through the pillars of leadership, a true leader moves beyond them to unyielding, undying *passion!* Couple this with a strong work ethic, a vision of growth, and total focus on your goals and fulfillment of purpose." St. James looked deep into Attila's eyes. "Do you have such vision, purpose, and passion?"

"Huh?"

The tall, gangly businessman twisted the lapel of his suit jacket. "I believe you do." St. James pulled a chunk of lamb from his souvlaki, picked it up with his fork, and chewed it slowly. He waited while his idea sank into its intended target. In the distance, a telephone rang at the cashier's desk. "I believe, at the moment, your vision is dormant, your purpose is hidden somewhere in your heart and brain. Yet their manifestations can be found in your love of languages. The power needed to generate fear and respect can be found in your passion for shooting and AK-47 reverence. These symbols of your character, personality traits, quirks, twists of heart and mind, can all be re-channeled into *leadership.* Greater self-knowledge is the key. If you use these potential strengths, along with persistence and a never-quit attitude, you'll lead our business to victory!"

Attila sat in silence. His right foot twitched, nervously pounding out a Turko-Mongolian rhythm.

"Why is leadership so scary?"

"Easy." The master businessman laid his fork beside his souvlaki plate. "Becoming a leader means championing your cause and accepting responsibility. Becoming a leader forces you to be your *best.* That means stepping out of your comfort zone. You rise to a higher level, enter a new energy plain."

Attila pushed his mega burger to the side. Squirming in Macedonian 7/8ths time, he sighed. "I'm not sure I can, or want, to do that."

"Not many people are," St. James continued. "It's a calling. Doubt is part of the process."

"Can't they call someone else?"

"That's what Moses said. And what a leader he turned out to be! Those born with the leadership gene ultimately cannot refuse the challenge. They become soldiers, warriors in the endless struggle between lethargy and freedom.

"As a leader, your followers will push you to fulfill your potential and climb the mountain of greatness. It's easy to retreat when you're only looking out for yourself. It's much harder when others depend on you to lead them."

Attila's listened. His mega burger remained untouched. "Lots to think about here," he concluded.

42

LEADERSHIP

S<small>T. JAMES LOOKED AROUND</small> the table. "Friends, explorers, Zanyite adventurers: Where do we begin?"

Scattered thoughts gathered in his brain. Finally, a powerful idea pushed through his trim-lipped mouth. "It's about fearless *leadership!*"

"Leadership is good," said Zany, brushing a wisp of gray hair from his eye. "As for fearless, I don't think so. I believe in fear. I trembled before each concert. Before I walked out on stage, sometimes for days in advance, I lived in quiet terror. I imagined the audience arriving with supplies of missiles: bottles, tomatoes, bananas, apples, oranges, heavy books, or other projectiles, to throw at me if I missed a note. Fear was my constant companion. It energized my fight for survival. Fear forced me to give my *best*."

St. James turned to his old friend. "But while you played, or savored your triumph after the concert, you felt *no* fear. Right?"

Zoltan considered. Twisting his memory mustache, he recalled his performance three years before of Ludwig Puffpott von Matterhorn's *Swiss Violin Concert in F major with the Alpine Symphony Orchestra.* "That is true."

The apostle leaned towards the doctor, driving home his point. "That's what fear-*less* means. Diving into your fear, working with its whirlwind energy. Eventually, you replace this vomititious, stomach-churning anxiety with a wonderful feeling of victory, strength, confidence, and joy."

"That's true, too."

St. James raised a bony finger towards a recessed light in the ceiling. Hammering in the concluding nail, he declared, "Pre-performance fears are normal. But you also had a higher calling: offering beautiful violin music to your audience, improving yourself, and, as the *tikkun olam* guys say, perfecting the world. Fear never disappears. But it can be conquered by a vision."

Zany applauded. "Well put. Bravo." From the sidelines, everyone nodded with approval.

President Attila rose from his seat. "An excellent summation! But here's the big question: if leadership is about vision, what is ours? What can our company do for others? How can we *use* whatever knowledge and skills we have to perfect the world? And, of course, to make money."

"Good question, my young friend. It points to the heart of our company. What do we do, and why bother doing it?"

"The business plan!" Teddy shouted. The volume of his enthusiasm startled the waitress three tables away. Diners surrounding them looked up, turned toward Teddy, and listened in anticipation. Teddy raised his hand and announced for all to hear, "Purpose! This is the cosmic meaning of our company."

Ghengis jumped up and grabbed Teddy's shoulder. The restaurant owner winced. "Our?" the Molecule snarled. "Since when did you become part of this?

"It's not official yet, but—"

Attila stepped in to calm the brewing tempest. "We'll settle membership problems later. At this point, we need *ideas*."

Teddy rubbed his aching shoulder while Ghengis picked up his fork, sank it into the table mat, and quietly resumed his seat.

The apostle continued, "The Zany Travel Company, Tour Company, whatever we want to call it, starts with Zany. It was his idea. If you want the reason for its formation, ask him."

"Me?" Zany looked surprised.

"Yes, you. Probe your deepest thoughts, your conscious and unconscious mind. Your son may be president, but you are the soul of this enterprise. Ask: What is the cosmic purpose of Zoltan Zany?"

An excited Attila turned to his father. "Pop, this *is* the big one. Mashugi would be proud. We'll find out why I went to Eastern Turkey searching for the Word. We may discover the meaning of life itself."

Zany fumbled. "Well. . . ?

The company president faced St. James. "Now I know why you're to top advisor for our group. *Koszonom szepen!"*

Martha's face reddened. "How dare you use that inferior Hungarian thank-you on him? *Danke shoen* is the simple, powerful way, and always superior."

"Don't get so hot, Martha. Teutonic languages are not my preference either. I'm a Finno-Ugric kind of guy."

"Stop bickering," Zany broke in.

"Okay," said Attila. "Let's move on. What's next?"

"We need an office," said Ghengis.

St. James was emphatic: "Before an office, we need a *program*. What will we do? Where will we go? Which itinerary shall we use?"

"Hungary is the home of my ancestors," said Zany. "It's the place to start."

"Hungary is a dump," Ghengis muttered. "Mongolia is better. Lots of open spaces."

"Germany is best," Martha stated. "Maybe even Austria."

"We could combine Germany, Austria, and Hungary into one tour," offered Attila. "We'll call it the 'Former Austrian-Hungarian Empire' tour."

Teddy looked at Zany and verbally elbowed his way in. "I like Tours to Hades."

Zany smiled. "I do, too. When I was a medical student in college, I had a similar idea."

Ghengis was unmoved. "Tours to Hades? Never work."

"I don't know." Attila considered it. "Indeed, the idea is preposterous. On the other hand, we are a Zany company. Preposterous is what we do."

"We can make it one part of our travel repertoire," said Zany. "We'll offer a choice: Present tours and future tours. Hungary or Hades. Tours for the living, and tours for the dead."

"Better to call them spiritual tours," said Teddy. "Even better, Tours of the Spirit."

"I see what you're saying." Zany stroked his chin as he pursued the concept further: "A place where the living meet the dead, and vice versa. But to call them Spiritual Tours has been done before. Too straight forward and boring. I've got a better name: *Posthumous Tours!*"

Martha disapproved. "What a hair-brained, insane scheme."

"Preposterous!" Ghengis snorted.

Stunned by this strange concept, the group fell silent. So did the diners listening in from the adjacent table. No one knew what to say.

After several minutes, St. James started to tap an Argentine tango rhythm on his plate with his finger nail. All eyes turned to him. The apostle studied the doubting eyes of his audience. He thought further. The tapping increased.

"Posthumous Tours may not be such a bad idea," he finally concluded. "Thinking as a businessperson, it's not as off-beat as it may sound. There's a large, untapped market out there. More people are dead than alive, after all. And, to my knowledge, none of them travel. Plus, here is the kicker: If reincarnation exists, there's an opportunity to start a new business: Selling insurance to Posthumous Tour travelers. We'll call it *Reincarnation Insurance*. *RI* for short. Instead of offering insurance money if you die, we'll offer it only if you *reincarnate*! A more liberal, but more expensive, policy would reimburse you if you reincarnated in *any* form. Our motto could be: 'It pays to live again!' There's lots of earnings potential here."

No one moved. The Xenophon Diner, famous for its commotion, noise, bustle, pots and pans banging in the back, occasional dishes crashing to the floor, waitresses shouting orders while tossing silverware on the table, was totally silent for the first time in its history. Even the pictures on the restaurant TV stopped.

Teddy's jaw dropped. He looked around the room. "I've never seen this before," he said. "It's a miracle."

Finally, Attila broke the silence. "How does this 'RI' work?

"Simple," St. James explained. "Before each tour, our travelers purchase RI insurance. When resurrection occurs—when they return, or are reborn—they get the money. If it doesn't, we keep the money. It's a win-win situation."

"This is crazy," Ghengis summarized.

Martha shook her head. "Totally incomprehensible."

"Complicated," Attila added.

St. James smiled. "Yes, it's crazy, incomprehensible, and complicated. It's totally zany. That's why it's perfect."

Teddy patted his chest. "Seems reasonable to me. And I agree that certainly Posthumous Tours *should* offer Reincarnation Insurance. Otherwise, there are no protections."

"This is all very interesting," said Attila. "But whether our tours are posthumous or not, we must ask: What will motivate others to travel with us? Why do people travel in the first place? Why bother leaving the comfort and security of your home?"

St. James turned the question a round in his mind. "Why travel?" he asked himself, before answering his own question. "Travel heals the mind, makes it whole. Not only do you travel for the cure, travel *is* the Cure! *Cur*-iosity: from the Latin root: *cura*, to care. Curiosity leads to cure, and vice versa. No germ can stand up to it. The triumvirate of curiosity, adventure, and fun chases disease away.

"The seventeenth-century Lithuanian Hassidic scholar, world traveler, linguist, and closet philosopher Cholek-ben-Jehudah-Holam-bar-Mitzvah-shel-Amit-Yochai-bat-Yam, of Vilna, known also as 'The Hebrew Hyphen,' called it the 'Tikkun Olam Cure.' Heal yourself, and you heal the world!"

PAYING THE BILLS

WHEN THE WAITRESS BROUGHT the check, Martha put a five-dollar bill on the table.

Ghengis reached into his pocket, then turned to the others. "I don't have any money. Cover me."

"That's disgusting, Ghengis," Martha growled. "Don't you *ever* carry money on you?"

"Never. It is not the Mongolian way."

"Screw the Mongolian way," Attila broke in. "To move ahead, we'll *need* money."

St. James chided Ghengis gently: "My Molecule, this is not a good business beginning." He opened his wallet. "I'll cover the bill for everyone this time," and said generously. "But tomorrow it will be different. Remember, money is vital in a Zany enterprise. Financial solvency is the most fundamental rule of all business. Before we open an office, we must ask: How do we finance this operation?"

"I'd worry about that later," said Teddy in opposition. "Make the move. Open the business whether you're financially solvent or not. That's how I started the Xenophon diner. First make your personal commitment. When you say *Yes!* to your dream, the cosmic forces line up for you. Progress and prosperity follow as Providence steps in to help you."

"There you go again," said St. James. "Don't forget to add work, sweat, toil, worry, and wonder."

"The Lord provides," Teddy insisted. "But, through a leap of faith, *we* must take the first step."

Zany looked pleased. "I'm beginning to like this guy. I admire the way he thinks. I believe he's right."

"What do you know about business?" snapped the saint. "Stick to your violin."

"Hey, I'll say what I want!" Zany shot back. "My son is president!"

Attila held up his hands. "Stop this! Give up this either- or. We'll do both: Deal with finance *and* open an office."

"Good idea," Teddy said. "The higher forces agree."

THE OFFICE

WEARING HIS NAVY BLUE corduroy etymology pants, Attila stood in reverential silence before the massive attic wall. Memories of his mother talking to virtual-chemical customers, coupled with his father's violin practice before an audience of forty paper dolls, peppered his mind.

"Could a Babylon of Hebrew be my destination?" he asked.

Deep bass echoes resonated within the wall as it answered, "Your destiny has yet to be written."

"I hear words clashing. Why do they haunt my mind?"

"Shivers of vibration in midget etymology form give syllabular hinting sounds of direction," the wall answered. "Fuse them together, and new roads will form. These hintings suggest your future path."

"You're smart."

"Yes, I'm a structure built for knowledge."

"Then tell me, why study languages? Why do I love them?"

"For their *music*. You're a sound man. Rather than the violin legacy of your father, you've chosen vocal cords. Vibrations resonate through your body as you speak. They unite lost elements in your scattered mind. The music of language brings oneness to your soul. It's healing, healthy, and wholesome—all from the same root, by the way."

Attila looked relieved.

"That's why you went to Mt. Ararat in search of the Word. Music of language is *you,* my boy. Linguistic vibrations inspire and motivate you. Music is the cardiac center of your family tradition. Your father and mother know it. The apostle knows it. Only you don't know it. Not yet, anyway. But soon you will. Bliss is hearing strange speech from mouths of foreigners. Attila, you're a xenophiliactic kind of guy."

Two months later, while he was studying in his attic studio, Attila heard the sound of brakes screeching to a halt. Looking out his window, he saw his father's 1989 Toyota pull into the driveway. Zany's violin case lay open in the back seat, although the violin itself was nowhere to be seen. Instead, the carcass of a Greek goat, with the legend *Destined for Gaidahood* pinned to its neck, lay inside the case.

Attila dropped a rock from his window. He had adopted this window-warning system from the medieval Crusader armies' mangonel catapult attacks against walled cities. As the rock crashed to the cement driveway beneath, Zany, realizing his son was home, looked up. When he spotted Attila's nose pressed against the window pane, he cupped his hands over his mouth and shouted, "Are you with book?"

Attila nodded.

"I met with St. James," said Zany. "Lots to talk about. I'm coming up." He removed a gold key from his pocket and opened the front door.

Zany's newly substantial form, fattened by months of sou-

vlaki and toned by an extensive weight-training regimen, entered the living room, checked out his mustache and flowing
white hair in the hallway mirror, and mounted the three flights
to the attic.

His son faced the wall. Annoyed, Zany shook his head and
growled, "Attila, you're talking again! You know how frustrat-
ing this can be."

But Attila looked relaxed, and happy. "Not at all, Father.
Bouncing ideas off my wall gives me feedback, self- understanding, even enlightenment. It costs less than a therapist, and it
works!"

"Your mother and I never approved. Trees are better. Why
can't you talk to them instead?"

"I need my own path."

"Your mother talks to plants. What about—"

"Trees, plants, whatever. My way is different." Attila
picked up his AK-47 from the bed and pointed it at the wall.
"Besides, if I don't like the answers, I can shoot them."

This Sicilian chess defense silenced his father. A pause ensued. Attila rearranged the papers on his desk, mopped the
floor, and pushed seven metal folding chairs into a circle.

"What are you doing?" Zany asked.

"Preparing our office."

"Office?"

"St. James insisted we watch our finances. You can't beat a
no-rent attic."

Stroking his right mandible, Zany considered this. "Good
idea. Not only do we save money, we never have to leave the
house."

Attila realized he had made his first presidential decision.
Panic gripped his belly. "Suddenly, my mind is totally blank."

"Fear of the definite," said Zany. "I know that phenomenon. It happened to me many times before I gave a concert."

"What did you do?" Attila paused. "Actually, Father, I don't care what *you* did. The real question is: What should *I* do?"

"Try hating others," Zany counseled.

"Isn't loving others better?"

"Love others, hate others—in the long run it really doesn't matter. Before my concerts, I used to focus on hating my audience. It got my mind off myself. After the concert, when my audience loved me, cheered me, and gave me a standing ovation, I loved them. So love or hate don't matter that much. Most important is to focus on something outside yourself. Just about anything will do." Zany watched his message sinking in. "Happiness begins with low expectations," he added. "It culminates, reaches its apotheosis, when you focus beyond yourself. This kind of higher focus increases self-control. It enables you to consider others, and thinking about others strengthens you."

Attila started practicing. He rose, faced the wall, and shouted, "I hate you!"

"Go for it!" Zany exclaimed.

The young etymologist seized the A-47, pointed it at the wall, and pulled the trigger. As round after round entered the plywood, he cried: "Take *that!* And *that!*" Bullet holes appeared in circular patterns. Furniture rattled. An oil painting of Rembrandt at his computer crashed to the floor. The sofa trembled, and the tulips in the vase expired.

When the fusillade ended, Attila quieted down. As the tension drained from his body, he collapsed in his fluffy armchair. "I feel so much better."

The lad put aside his gun. A look of peace and satisfaction crossed his face. With the assumption of presidential responsibiolity, the need to fire his AK-47 drained out of him.

"First comes relaxation, then comes focus," said his father. "Or is it vice versa? I'm not sure. In any case, the important thing is that, as president of this enterprise, you are ready to chair our staff meeting."

"You mean right *now?*"

"Yes. You made a good judgment call. The attic is our best office space. I agreed with you a few days ago, even before you had enough self-knowledge to agree with yourself. So without your presidential permission, I took it upon myself to arrange a staff meeting. Our staff will all be here at 10:00 this morning."

"But it's 9:30 now," said Attila, anxiously checking his watch. "They'll be here in half an hour!"

"Right. But only if they come on time."

As recollection of presidential responsibilities flooded his brain, Attila stiffened with resolve. Lines of strength hardened at his jaw. He straightened, stood tall, threw back his shoulders, and, following Zany traditions of the past, stamped a power-fully organized, determined left foot. "Tardiness will not be *tolerated!* Our staff will always be on time. Otherwise, they will no longer *be* our staff!"

Zany's eyebrows rose in satisfaction. "Very impressive. Such leadership qualities in my own son!"

Attila lowered his gun. "I owe it to Isaac Mashugi, etymol-ogy, Mount Ararat, and Noah's Ark." He aimed his AK-47 at the ceiling and pulled the trigger. He gazed at the holes in the ceiling, lapsed into a silent meditation, and in time, reverently, added, "This is only the beginning."

PAST REFLECTIONS

NCE AGAIN, ZANY WAS sitting in his armchair. President Attila sat on the sofa opposite him. Glass of water in hand,
feet extended and resting on a footstool, awe and wonder descended upon the violinist as he considered the inner processes
of his mind. How did it work, after all? How had he, a concert
artist, come up with the entrepreneurial idea of Posthumous
Tours? As he reflected, he slipped back into memories and personal history. He recalled a vision he'd had at fourteen. In it,
he had led a tour to Hungary.

However, due to parental pressure, and his love of music, he
had pushed this travel and leadership vision into the back-
ground. Instead, he had chosen to became a violinist both to
please the musical elf, a fantasy figure named Juan the Spinach
Span-Yard (who dwelled in a childlike place in his cerebellum),
and to fulfill the musical hopes of his mother, an adoring fan of
Mozart. The sound of Zany wailing in his crib had caused her
musical dream to swell and culminate in ecstatic chemical weep-
ing and metaphysical happiness when, in later years, she heard
him practicing Lalo's *Symphonie Espangnol.*

Zany's father had been more of a adventurer. A masterpiece

of curiosity, he'd had an open-minded business approach and entrepreneurial zest for the mystery of travel.

Although Papa Zany worked as a high school history teacher, his unfulfilled life's dream was to build a Travel Empire. Like his hero, Orpheus—the Thracian musician, poet, and son of the Thracian King Oeagrus—Papa Zany wanted to travel, not only in this world, but in the next.

Like any Thracian, he worshiped the horse and believed in reincarnation. Like every Thracian, he cried at the birth of every new child because he knew that entrance into this world brought only pain, and he celebrated funerals, rejoicing in the delivery of the pain-wracked soul of the deceased into the Land beyond Suffering and the bliss of afterlife.

Papa Zany traveled mostly on horseback, riding in upstate New York, where he owned a small ranch, subsidized by a large vegetable garden and local tulip and broccoli sales. It was the Zany family's summer getaway home located on seventy-five acres in Ham-done. On that upstate retreat, Papa Zany rode his steed, Philip-the-Horse, down country roads every summer.

He refused to travel any other way. When asked about fulfilling his dream of visiting his Magyar homeland, he would reply, "I love to gallop, and when my horse Philip can cross the ocean, I'll visit Hungary.

Zany's father was a man of unfulfilled dreams. He often claimed defiantly, "I don't have time to fulfill my dreams. Let Zoltan fill them for me. That's what sons are for."

Papa Zany had built a shrine for Philip facing the brook and mountains behind the ranch. There, every morning before sunrise, he had prayed to his pantheon of equine gods.

"I don't know much about history," Attila said, gazing at

his father. "Yet when I read about it, hear the names and sounds of those exotic foreign places, tribes, and cities, my mind goes wild."

"It's true, you are historically ignorant," his father confirmed. "Yet you were born in a musical family. Naturally, the sounds of the wild spots increase the blood flow to your imagination. Going wild is a Zany characteristic. In our family tradition, some have syphoned their wild side into music; others, like you, express it through etymology and historical sounds; and some, like Papa Zany, merely dream about it by picturing foreign lands and distant travel adventures. A free-roaming imagination is a Zany trait. It's perfectly reasonable that you should be so afflicted."

Zany reached into a dresser drawer and pulled out a tattered manuscript. He fondled it gently in his hands, letting pieces of ancient, crinkled parchment fall to the floor. "Here's a scrap from *Journals of Papa Zany*," he said. "I know you'll appreciate what he said in 1847 and repeated in 1947."

Zany donned his reading glasses.

> *Max the Triballian from Vratsa likes to write.*
> *Why? He is a fool of valor playing with history.*
> *Mysian competition with later Roman Moesia came down strong. Imagination took a sidewalk as sandwiches roped off local alleys, releasing mental madness throughout the empire.*
> *Now freedom flies everywhere.*

"Sounds like gibberish to *me*," Attila declared.

"Perhaps, but that too is a Zany trait. Through gibberish and babble, we often make discoveries about the human condition and our place in it."

Attila reflected upon his father's explanation. "Sounds wise," he concluded.

"It *is* wise. Papa Zany was a smart cocker."

"Then history, with its etymological curves, is the doorway to my imagination?" Attila asked as he summarized.

"Yes," Zany answered. "Attila, my son, you are the student among us. The scholar and intellectual. I suggest you start studying reincarnation and the afterlife. Begin with the Thracians."

Zany sat back in his armchair, took a sip of water, and continued reflecting on his past. "Ah, I remember my Thracian concert tour! The towns of Drama in northern Greece, and Zagora in Eastern Bulgaria, were the best! Standing ovations everywhere. What applause! Those Thracians know how to clap. And they have a special way of doing it by striking the palm of their left hand with the four fingers of their right. An explosive sound ensues, like the crack of a whip. Put clapping Thracians in a concert hall, and, if they love your playing, thunderous ovations come out! My musical hero, Orpheus, was a Thracian. I model much of my rubato and musical phrasing after his flute playing. Too bad about losing Euridice. Maybe he missed a note."

Attila listened attentively. "I like studying the ancient Greeks. I could add the Thracians. I've been having trouble writing in my etymological journal lately. Perhaps their musicianship and belief in the afterlife might move me along. You're right, Pop. Study fills my mind with confidence and ideas. Researching the Thracians might even help us develop our Posthumous Tours. Yes, reincarnation and the afterlife—along with study of ancient Greek mythology, history, and geography—will be something new for me. I'd add Thrace, and who knows what else? All this will infuse me with new purpose. Perhaps I'll even learn Hebrew and explore life in ancient Israel. Any reincarnation and afterlife connections there?"

THE ATTIC BUSINESS PLAN

A T THE FIRST MEETING in the new attic office, St. James stood before the group. In one hand, he held a piece of paper with notes scribbled all over it, in the other a conductor's baton.

"In my left hand, I hold our business plan; in my right, an orchestral baton, symbol of our company and its tour leadership. We shall divide our enterprise into two parts. Our first area, short-range endeavor, deals with the present. We'll call it Present Tours. Our second area, long-range endeavor, deals with the future. This will be Posthumous Tours." The Apostle nodded to Attila, who clicked a button on his computer console and projected a PowerPoint slide against the far wall that read:

1. Destinations and itineraries of Present Tours.

2. Destinations and itineraries for Posthumous Tours.

a. Destinations: Past Tour: Roman Empire Tour, Holy Roman Empire Tour (Medieval Sites, etc.)

b. Future tours: Mars, Saturn with Pluto extension.

"Thanks, Mr. President," St. James continued. "Now, here's how we can make money with Posthumous Tours. In fact, *the best* way to make money in this present world, during our existence in material reality, is by creating a new product or service, one that has never existed before. This financial product will be: Reincarnation Insurance.

"I explained it before, but let me repeat it. If our customers buy Reincarnation Insurance (RI) and reincarnation exists, then after they return from their sojourn in Hades, hell, heaven, limbo, or wherever else they go, they collect on their policy. If, on the other hand, reincarnation does *not* exist, then we keep the premiums.

"For example, we sell a $50,000 RI policy for $1,000 to a traveler. If they reincarnate, they collect $50,000. If reincarnation does not exist, and they do not return, we have earned $1,000."

Attila shrugged. "I believe in reincarnation," he said, "but recognition would present a problem. When our clients return to collect, how do we know it is really them? How can we know they are the formerly dead who bought the policy?"

"Ah, *you* are very *clever*," St. James replied. "Here's the answer. The plan is scam proof. Upon their return, our travelers will have to *prove* they purchased the policy, that they indeed lived their past lives. They will need, not only the Reincarnation Insurance certificate we give them when they take out the insurance, but other forms of identification as well: Pre-existence passports, drivers licenses, social security numbers, home addresses, telephone numbers, email addresses. . .in other words, travelers *can* collect, but it won't be easy. We don't want just *any* body, soul, or spirit trying to collect."

POSTHUMOUS TOURS

ANY RUBBED HIS HANDS together gleefully. Smiling with satisfaction, he announced the new Posthumous Tours marketing slogan: *"No Body Travels With Us!"*

Standing on one foot to illustrate the company message, he expanded further: "Put your daily existence on a firm foundation. Place one foot in this life and one foot in the next. Look forward to your future! A posthumous tour with us is an incomparable adventure. It will free you from anxiety, instill a positive attitude, and give you a long-term perspective in both this life and the next."

The business consultants sat in a circle, appreciating Zany's exposition of the PT philosophy. Martha and St. James applauded. Ghengis nodded vigorously.

"Can you go to hell?" Teddy asked.

"We'll go anywhere," Zany answered proudly.

Attila asked, "Which is better, heaven or hell?"

"During my concert tours, I discovered that all destinations have something interesting to offer."

St. James stepped in. "These are irrelevant questions. The

real question is, Which itinerary will draw the most customers? Will heaven attract more clients, or do most people want to go to hell? At the moment, we don't know."

Attila let this cosmic concept of business savvy seep into his brain. "I agree," he said. "Before we move ahead, we need more market research and analysis."

"Correct!" Zany concurred, lighting his newly acquired businessman's pipe. As the wood started to burn, he dipped it into his glass of water.

"Stop that!" Martha slapped his hand. "If you're going to smoke that thing, at least put tobacco in first!"

"I'm still learning," the doctor insisted. "Smoking is a new habit for me. I need it to impress customers."

"Smoking went out of fashion twenty years ago," said Genghis. "These days, only Mongolians smoke."

"Mongolians have grabbed the titanium market," Attila put in. "They've cornered most of the rare earth metals, too. Maybe we should all learn to smoke."

St. James raised a warning finger. "Smoking is a distraction. So are rare earth metals. We already have our specialty, our niche market. We need to focus on our strengths, our areas of growth—such as death and resurrection. How can we sell and promote our new business? How can we turn our company into a success? Rare metals, what is in the earth, are not our concern. Our most important question is: Who is *under* the earth. That's our customer base."

"Our customers also dwell in the heavenly abode," added Teddy. "Many former Xenophon diners are there today."

"Customers, customers! It sounds so crass." The inner peace of college days, word origins, and etymological study flashed through Attila's mind. "Can't you think of anything else?"

Zany answered in a fatherly tone: "My son, let me remind you that, without customers, there is no business. End of argument. Onward, upward, and sideward!"

St. James arose. "Before we adjourn this meeting, I have a concluding thought." The apostle spoke with finality. "Our company is young. Yet even at this early stage, I believe it has gone far enough. We have gone as far as we can go."

"But we're just starting," protested Genghis.

"He's joking," said Teddy.

Attila looked baffled. ". . .No, I think he's serious."

"I just baked some doughnuts of the Austrian variety," Martha announced. "I'll fetch them from the kitchen."

Zany looked at his friend. "Why are you saying that? What do you mean?"

"Easy," St. James responded. "Posthumous Tours is not about tomorrow, next week, next year, or next decade. It is about the long-term future."

"That's true," Attila agreed. "We're planning ahead."

"Yes," answered the Apostle, "far ahead. We're posthumous planners. And that is precisely the problem. We can't go any further until we die."

Ghengis ground his teeth, Attila bit his nails, Teddy folded his hands in his lap, and Zany thought about violin notes floating in space. They all sat in silence, pondering this insight.

St. James continued, "Our company is about unfinished business. As the Bulgarians say, 'When building a house, always leave a room unfinished.' We are leaving rooms unfinished, giving space for future explorations and growth. This growth can only be finished in the future."

Zany sighed and nodded. "Spoken like a true sage. Very wise indeed."

"But is it?" asked Attila. "Unlike you old birds, I'm young. I've got space and time in my life. I want to do something *now!*"

Genghis looked glum. "How disappointing. I was hoping we could make some money. I'd like to visit Mongolia again in my present body. In fact, I just booked a flight to Ulan Bator for next weekend."

"Nice," said St. James. "Traveling in your present body, is a good idea. Very healthy. For this life. But we're talking *future.*"

"I'm starting my future next week," Genghis boasted.

"I can't wait either," Attila exclaimed. "I'm ordering a *Sanskrit Etymological Dictionary* tomorrow!"

"In terms of minutes, tomorrow is small change," Zany pointed out. "You're just like your mother, always in a rush."

The group fell silent. Hours passed as they contemplated the great questions. Finally, Zany whispered, "A deep exhaustion is gnawing every bone. I felt the same depletion at the end of my concert career. I had gone as far as I could go. My bones told me to put career aside, transition, do something different, reinvent myself as something new. My bones are speaking again. They're trying to convince me to sideline our company for awhile. Let it wait and cook. St. James is right. At least for now, we can't go any further. Let's take a vacation. Time is our greatest illusion. We'll wake up refreshed. Then we can continue growing our company."

Martha flicked a doughnut crumb off her glasses. "You have a point. And by then the coffee will be ready."

"Proper hydration is important," Attila declared.

As his decision crystallized, Zany continued, "It's too early to organize and grow Posthumous Tours."

"Why is that?" asked Attila.

Dr. Zany rose before answering. "The Apostle is right. It's so obvious, I don't know why I didn't think of it before. Posthumously Tours can only be organized *posthumously.*"

"So you'll have to wait until you're dead?"

"Exactly."

Attila thought it over. "Well, it's true that, with your soul lost in space, boredom might set in. This can be a problem, even in the afterlife. Building your company posthumously will give you something constructive and creative to do."

"Absolutely correct. I'll start by conferring with Mother Zany on travel. She's good at that."

"You'll find lots of cheap help beyond."

"Yes. And there won't be any union problems either!"

"So let us all agree," Zany summarized. "We'll put our company on hold for awhile. We'll get back to it some time in the future. We'll even set our next meeting date. How is Thursday, October 2, 2106?"

St. James shook his head. "Autumn is a season of decline. Spring is better. Let's do Monday, March 23, 2307."

After a few more hours of contemplation, the entire staff agreed as well. Zany postponed the development of Posthumous Tours until the arrival of infinity.

www.ingramcontent.com/pod-product-compliance
Lightning Source LLC
Chambersburg PA
CBHW050515260626
47157CB00004B/1331